Country Stars in Maple Bay

A Maple Bay Novel, Book 3

Brittney Joy

Contents

Newsletter Invitation

MAPLE BAY SERIES:
Rescued in Maple Bay (prequel)
Starting Over in Maple Bay (book 1)
Second Chance in Maple Bay (book 2)
Country Stars in Maple Bay (book 3)
Matched in Maple Bay (book 4)

Sign up for Brittney's newsletter – stay in touch and never miss a new release!
http://www.brittneyjoybooks.com/newsletter

Dedicated to my Prince Charming.
You are my happily-ever-after.

Chapter One

Myra had twenty minutes to get to the bank and fix the mess she'd created. But instead of rushing out the door, she was swirling whipped cream on a peppermint mocha.

"Here you go, Eleanor." Myra passed the warm mug over the counter. She knew her regulars' favorites by heart. Eleanor started every morning with a peppermint mocha. Even when it was scorching hot outside.

"Thank you, sweets." Eleanor winked at Myra. Then she carried her mocha to the other side of the Perkup Coffee shop, where she joined a table of cackling ladies—all well into their seventies. The ladies gathered at the shop most mornings to share coffee, laughter, and an array of gossip. Myra had learned long ago that if she wanted to know who'd sped down Main Street or what casserole so-and-so had brought to the potluck, she simply needed to eavesdrop on Eleanor and her friends for five minutes.

Today she didn't need gossip. She needed a miracle.

Myra wiped down the counter and strode to the back of the shop. Her ten-year-old son, Finch, sat in the corner booth with Pete and Hal, two retired policemen.

"Hey, Mom!" Finch called from the booth. "Want to see the new magic trick Hal taught me?"

"Sure, Finchy." Myra wiped her still-damp hands on her turquoise apron, welcoming the innocent distraction.

Finch made a quarter *magically* appear from behind Hal's ear. "Isn't that awesome?" Her son's eyes were big as the saucer under Hal's coffee cup. Hal and Pete chuckled at his enthusiasm.

"Totally awesome." Myra grinned and mussed her son's hair. Then her mind snapped back to the task at hand. "Has your sister made an appearance yet?" Myra glanced at the clock on the wall. Seven-forty. The school bus would be outside the coffee shop in ten minutes.

Finch shrugged. "Not yet." Then he leaned over and made a quarter appear behind Hal's ear again. He giggled with amusement.

"Get your backpack, Finchy." Myra headed down the hall toward the back door. The short hall spurred off to a small office on one side and a staircase on the other. The stairs led upstairs to where Myra and her kids lived. "Paisley, let's go!" Myra called, starting up the stairs.

The door at the top of the stairs opened, and Paisley appeared. Her face did not look particularly sweet. Paisley was barely fifteen, and sometime in the last year, hormones had snuck into her body and turned her previously calm disposition into a rollercoaster of teenage emotions. This morning, it seemed like she was on a downward spiral.

"The bus is going to be here soon. Come on."

Paisley started down the stairs, pushing her long ebony hair behind her shoulder. "Can't you just give us a ride to school?"

"I already told you I can't." Irritation sharpened Myra's tone, but she took a deep breath and tried not to kick off World War III. Paisley was a mini-Myra. They both had short fuses. Sometimes that meant they blew up at each other, and Myra didn't have the energy to smooth over an explosion. "Not today."

"But I'm like the oldest person on the bus. So not cool." Paisley sighed and shuffled down the stairs. "Grandma can't take us?"

"She's at a doctor's appointment."

"Becca?" Paisley pressed, referring to Myra's single employee. "You said she'd be here soon."

"She will." Myra zoned in on her daughter, giving her a look that warned her not to continue down the road she was on. "She's taking care of the shop while I run some errands. She can't take you to school either."

Paisley stopped in front of Myra. "Can I at least make a smoothie?" she asked, as if a smoothie was the only thing that would keep her from dying.

"You haven't eaten yet?" Myra raised an eyebrow but decided not to pick this battle either. "Hurry. You've got exactly five minutes to whip one together."

Paisley cracked a small grin. "Thanks. I'll be fast."

Myra followed her daughter back into the shop and grabbed a carafe. She topped off Pete and Hal's mugs, and when she stepped back behind the counter, Paisley had a blender filled with ice, milk, yogurt, and a banana. She was adding a splash of orange juice to her concoction when she got distracted by something out the front window. She set the jug of juice on the counter.

"What is *that*?" Paisley asked like a spaceship had just zoomed by.

"What is what?" Myra looked up, hoping to find Becca entering the shop. Instead, she laid eyes on a fancy sports car that had parked directly in front of the coffee shop. Its cobalt-blue paint glittered like a jewel.

Myra squinted. Who the heck was driving that fancy-dancy thing? A couple thousand people lived in Maple Bay, and Myra knew most all of them. Most she'd grown up with. No one drove anything that resembled that car. *What is that—a Porsche?*

The driver's door opened, and Myra's suspicions were confirmed. No one she knew.

Shiny boots and long, jean-clad legs stepped out and onto the sidewalk. A man close to her age, maybe forty, stood tall. She couldn't believe he fit in such a tiny car.

"Huh," Myra said, mostly to herself, reluctantly admiring his wide shoulders and strong arms. They were hard to miss, even under a baby-blue Henley. Then she furrowed her brow, trying to get a look at his face. That was nearly impossible due to black sunglasses and a baseball hat pulled low.

"That guy looks familiar," Paisley said with a cock of her head, like she was trying to place him.

"What do you mean, *familiar*?" Myra was ready to grill Paisley, but her curiosity quickly melted to confusion when the car's passenger door swung open. A man in a suit appeared: Chad. The same man Myra was supposed to meet at the bank this morning.

Myra made a choking sound.

"Mom?" Paisley asked. "You okay?"

She blinked, trying to make sense of what was happening. "I . . ." Myra cleared her throat. "Yeah, of course. Finish making your smoothie."

Paisley put away the orange juice as both men entered the coffee shop. Chad walked through the door first. The other man followed.

"Hey, Chad," Myra greeted. "I thought I was going to meet you at the bank. Eight o'clock, right?"

A tight smile inched across Chad's face. Myra didn't like the look of it.

"Sorry about that, Myra. I've got some news and wanted to talk to you as soon as possible. In person." He looked around. "And in private."

"Okay. Let me get my kids out the door first. The bus will be here any minute." Myra looked over her shoulder for Finch, but he was nowhere to be found. "Paisley, can you go get your brother? He must've run upstairs to grab his backpack."

Paisley looked less than enthusiastic about Myra's request, but left to fetch Finch.

"Can I get you and your friend a coffee while you wait?" Myra asked, eyeing Chad's *friend*, who was glancing around the shop, sizing it up. He still wore his sunglasses even though spring showers drizzled outside.

"No, that's okay. We've already had coffee," Chad replied.

"This used to be an old barn?" the man asked. Myra wasn't sure if he was talking to her or to Chad.

"Used to be," she confirmed. It still resembled a barn. Except instead of dairy cows, the wooden floors supported tables, chairs, coffee makers, and an espresso machine. "I renovated it when I bought the place a few years ago."

The man's attention fell to her, though she still couldn't see past the dark lenses that covered his eyes.

"What year was it built?" he asked, stone-faced.

Myra wanted to ask if it was too sunny for him inside the shop. Instead, she said, "Nineteen thirty-six."

"Interesting," the man replied, crossing one muscled arm over the other.

Who was this guy? Was he from the bank as well?

"I'm sorry, I didn't get your name." Myra reached over the counter, offering her hand for him to shake.

The man hesitated for a few seconds, like he'd forgotten who he was. Then he stepped forward and shook Myra's hand. "Skyler."

A sharp squeak sounded from behind Myra. She let go of Skyler's hand and twisted to find Paisley behind her, her eyes wide.

"What's wrong?" Myra asked, her gaze darting behind Paisley to search for Finch.

"That's . . ." Paisley stuttered. "That's Skyler Ridge." She couldn't have sounded more astonished if she'd discovered gold floating in her smoothie.

"Paisley," Myra gently scolded. "Close your mouth and get your head on straight. Nobody like that comes here." Myra turned back toward the front of the shop, intending to brush off her daughter's accusation with a chuckle, but when she looked at Chad and Skyler, they weren't laughing.

In fact, Paisley's accusation pushed Chad to step in close. He leaned over the counter and whispered to Myra. "I really need to talk to you. In private."

Myra's body temperature dropped. What was going on here? She looked back at Sunglasses Man. He *did* kind of look like the singer. Minus the telltale beard. But, no . . . it couldn't be.

Out of the corner of her eye, Myra caught sight of the yellow school bus slowing to a stop in front of the shop.

"Kids!" she called, even though she knew Paisley was right behind her. "Time to go."

Without looking, Myra reached out and turned on the blender, intending to hurry her daughter out the door with her smoothie. The blender whirled to life, and its contents erupted like a miniature volcano. Myra jerked as milk, yogurt, and orange juice attacked her. Globs dripped down the walls and pooled on the counter and floor. Myra lurched for the blender through the splattering and managed to turn off the appliance, but not before everyone standing close to the counter was dripping in peachy sludge.

"Oh," Myra breathed. "For Pete's sake." Orange goop dripped down her front. She licked her bottom lip, sucking in a dollop of yogurt. On the other side of the counter, Chad and Skyler were also doused in smoothie. They held their hands in the air like she'd threatened to rob them.

Myra quickly turned and snatched a stack of towels from a cabinet. As she did, her eyes met Paisley's.

"Oops." Paisley looked stunned. Her hands were also raised, and she was holding the top of the blender.

Myra thought about strangling her daughter. But no, that would only drag out this already disastrous day. "Oops is right." The only silver lining was that Myra's body had shielded Paisley from the flying sludge. "Grab a banana. The bus is waiting for you."

"Sorry, Mom." Paisley took a banana and backed out from behind the counter.

Just then, Finch ran into the shop, his backpack bouncing against his back. "Whoa!" He skidded to a stop. "What happened to you?"

"Smoothie explosion." Myra wiped her face with a towel and shooed both kids toward the door. "I'll see you after school. Take the bus home."

This time, Paisley didn't complain.

As the kids scooted out the door, Myra approached Chad and Skyler. She handed a towel to each of them, keeping one for herself.

"I'm so sorry," she said. "I should've checked the top before I turned it on." Myra reached for Skyler and patted a towel over his shirt, sopping up the mess. He froze at her touch.

When Myra realized what she was doing, she stiffened as well. Her hand stopped, pressed against his chest. *A very solid chest.* Was he made of wood? For the briefest second, she thought about knocking on his pectoral to make sure.

She glanced up. Orange slop and banana bits colored his black sunglasses and clean-shaven jawline. He quirked an eyebrow. Then he slid the glasses from his face, exposing hazel—nearly copper—eyes. For a beat, she got trapped in them.

"I think I got it," he said. Without the glasses, Skyler looked a tad amused . . . and familiar. A gear turned in Myra's head.

It is *him.*

The playful smirk. The eyes that had charmed one too many actresses out of their senses. His face was unmistakable. She'd seen it plastered all over the tabloids. *Especially lately.* She just hadn't recognized him without the scruffy beard.

Myra jerked her hand from his chest, cursing her mom reaction. What was she doing? He wasn't a toddler. She didn't need to wipe him down.

"Honey, you okay? You need some help?" Eleanor called from across the shop. All four ladies were getting up out of their chairs, ready to come to Myra's rescue.

Myra snapped out of her stupor. "I'm okay, Eleanor. Don't get up." She flicked her wrist like it was no biggie that she was standing in her coffee shop dripping in smoothie slop.

"Looks like your customers got a little more than they asked for." Eleanor good-naturedly chuckled. "Next time, ask for coffee," she called to Chad and Skyler.

Chad did not look amused by Eleanor's humor. He dabbed frantically at his suit.

Skyler managed a grin. "Next time, I'll order the coffee."

Eleanor winked at Skyler and sat back down to continue her gossip. Little did she know a big, juicy piece of gossip was standing fifteen feet from her.

"Why are you here?" Myra asked bluntly. She could've directed her question at Chad or at Skyler. For the time being, it was meant for the famous country music star. "In Maple Bay?" she clarified.

Skyler grabbed the brim of his baseball cap, pulling it back before giving his face a once-over with the towel Myra had given him. Myra kept her eyes on him as she also cleaned herself up, blotting smoothie from her shirt and apron.

He stuffed his baseball hat back over chestnut locks. "Looking for some peace and quiet."

She couldn't tell if he was joking. "In northern Minnesota? Don't you live in Nashville?"

"Something like that," he replied.

Chad burst into their conversation like he had somewhere to go—probably a shower. "Myra, can we go somewhere to talk? Privately?"

"Sure." Myra knew what she had to talk to Chad about. She was behind on her mortgage, but she'd been busting her butt for months. She'd saved up a good chunk of money and could write the bank a check today to cover a few of the back payments. "How about the patio?"

Chad nodded, and Myra led them down the short hall and out the back door. Perkup Coffee was at the far end of Main Street. It was the last business on the main drag—which consisted of three blocks, meaning the shop was mostly surrounded by residential houses. The backyard butted up to a gravel alleyway and was split down the middle. Half of the yard held a wooden patio area with tables and chairs. A fence edged the other half. Every now and then, Myra liked to ride her horse to work, but the fenced area was empty today.

"Have a seat," Myra offered, glad the rain had let up. She meandered to the first table, which was under the cover of an umbrella. "I know I'm late, but I can write you a check today for . . ." She was about to pull out a chair and sit when she realized Skyler had followed Chad. Myra stilled, her hand on the chair. "Uh, this"—she pointed between her chest and Chad's—"is definitely a private conversation. Feel free to help yourself to anything inside. There's hot coffee in the carafe on the counter."

"Did I misunderstand something?" Skyler asked, looking confused. He shot a look at Chad.

"Uh, no. You didn't. Misunderstand, that is." Chad stumbled over his words.

"Chad," Myra interjected. "What's going on?"

"The bank sold Perkup." Chad's words slipped out of his mouth like they'd been greased.

He might as well have just punched her on the chin. Myra cranked her head to the side. "The. Bank. Did. What?" Her mind had slowed to the point at which she could only get one word out at a time.

"Look, Myra. You've been behind in payments for over six months. I warned you this would happen. That your shop would go into foreclosure. I tried to tell you."

"But I said I would make it up." She stared at Chad. Was she having a bad dream? Could she wake up? This was *her* shop. *Her* livelihood. *Her* home.

"I couldn't stop it. The bank got an offer, and sold it this week-end," Chad said, the words quiet and apologetic.

"Just like that? They sold my shop just like that?" Myra's breathing turned to heaving. "Some stranger bought my shop? And my house?"

"You live here?" Skyler asked abruptly.

Myra ignored him. She kept her focus on Chad. "Who would buy my shop? Naomi? Oh, that little . . . buying up her competition?" Heat rose up her throat and into her cheeks. If Naomi had snatched up her shop, Myra would run across town and strangle that floozy herself.

Chad swallowed. He shook his head. "Naomi didn't buy it."

A long, bizarre pause stretched out between them. Myra stared, her brain slowly sifting through the clues.

Then she whirled around and pointed at Skyler. "You bought my shop?"

Chapter Two

Skyler had been chased by plenty of rabid fans. Usually women with stars in their eyes and a determination that was tricky to contain, even with security. But as he stood on the patio behind the coffee shop he'd just bought, Myra glared at him with an intensity he wasn't sure he'd ever seen. If she'd had pistols behind her turquoise eyes, he'd have been riddled with bullets by now.

"You . . ." Myra took a breath. "Stole my shop?"

"Stole?" The question rolled off Skyler's tongue in disbelief. He'd bought Perkup Coffee from the bank, fair and square. He considered reminding Myra that she'd let her business fall into foreclosure. However, he wasn't certain of her sanity and didn't want to make the situation worse.

Skyler lifted his hands, offering surrender. "Look, maybe I should step away and let you two talk." He took a step back, wondering why Chad had brought him to the shop this morning.

Skyler had had no idea Myra was still running the business. Hadn't the bank repossessed the shop last month?

"I think that's a great idea," Myra said, practically steaming. She crossed her arms over her chest and squared up like a brick wall.

This was not how he'd seen this morning going. Last week, after the tabloids had gotten a hold of some information that had caused his music career to implode, his agent had practically begged him to lie low. Which was how he'd ended up in Maple Bay. Had he run from one disaster just to be thrown into another?

"I've got the money," Myra said to Chad. "I can write you a check for two months' payments right now."

"Myra," Chad replied, "I told you last week that wasn't going to work. You're too far behind on your payments. The bank wanted you to be up to date a month ago."

Myra's mouth opened and closed, but no words came out. Skyler backed away, needing to get out of this conversation. He took two steps before Chad stopped him.

"No, wait. Stay, please," Chad said. "There's a reason I brought you with me today."

Skyler stopped. What kind of insane explanation would Chad give for the mess he'd thrown together?

"I wanted you two to meet," Chad continued. "Skyler will need someone to manage Perkup. And I thought maybe the two of you could work something out. Something beneficial for you both. I thought that might help you through this transition." His last sentence was directed at Myra.

"Transition?" She looked dumbfounded. "Chad, you just told me that I lost my coffee shop. My livelihood. The place my kids call home. A place I've been working my butt off for. And you just expect me to turn around and agree to work for some hotshot celebrity that stole my shop out from under me? I don't . . . I just don't . . ."

Myra's armor seemed to fall away. Her anger wavered. The intensity in her eyes went glassy.

Oh, crap. Was she going to cry?

Skyler wished he'd already left. His insides cringed. He didn't want to be the source of pain.

"Look, I think I'm going to wait in the car." He took another step back.

Myra quickly wiped her hands over her eyes, pushing away tears and what was left over from the smoothie. "Why do you want this place? What are you going to do with it?" She waved her hand at the shop. At him.

He didn't know this woman, and he certainly wasn't going to tell her the truth. The last time he'd told a woman his secrets, she'd sold them to the tabloids. And look how that had turned out.

"It's an investment," he replied.

"An investment?" Myra's response was quieter than her previous questions. "Skyler Ridge is investing in a no-name coffee shop in the tiny town of Maple Bay? Why? I can think of plenty of businesses that would be more profitable."

"I don't think it's any of your business what I—"

Myra didn't let him finish. "To you, this shop might look like dollar signs. I'm sure you picked it up for a steal, and maybe you think you can spruce it up and resell it. Make a quick dollar. But do you want to know what this shop means to me?"

Skyler's mouth was still open from when he'd tried to reply to her the first time. He closed it.

"To me, this shop gave me independence when I had to pick myself up off the floor and start over. It supports me and my kids. It's a roof over our heads. It's a lot more than dollar signs." Myra's eyes went glassy again, and she didn't wait for a reply. Instead, she walked past Skyler and into the coffee shop. Her long black ponytail swayed against her back, punctuating her exit.

As the door slammed shut behind her, Skyler looked back at Chad, guilt and irritation rising in his chest. "You could have warned me what we were walking into. I probably would've stayed at the bank and let you handle this."

Chad looked defeated. He blew out a sigh. "She really is a nice lady."

Skyler quirked an eyebrow, remembering the death glare Myra had just given him.

Chad sat on the edge of a table. "I didn't want to see this happen. I mean, I tried to give her every chance possible to get current on her loan, but she just couldn't do it. I hate to see her in this position." He tapped his fingers on the table. "Would you be open to offering her a job? Letting her rent out the second floor? I know she didn't seem too keen on the idea just now, but I'll talk to her about it."

Chad was staring at him like he could be Myra's savior. Skyler got that look a lot. Most people thought he could solve all their problems through money or fame. Like he was a doctor ready to hand out happy pills in the form of dollars.

"I don't know." Skyler itched to put his sunglasses back on and drive out of here. He'd come back once Chad had cleaned up this mess.

"She is honestly the hardest worker I've ever seen. She's just been through some hard times and couldn't pull herself out of the hole. She's a single mother with two kids. You saw them."

Skyler's stomach clenched. Chad had to pull out the kid card? Of course he'd seen them. He was trying not to think too hard about that. "I was going to bring in a manager from out of town. I've got a recruiter contacting candidates already."

Chad grimaced. "That might be a hard sell."

"Hard sell? To whom?"

"To Maple Bay. This is a tight-knit community. They support local, and if you bring in an out-of-towner to replace Myra, that might not go over well."

Skyler didn't know how long he'd keep the shop. He didn't know how long he'd stay in Maple Bay. But for the time being, he didn't want to create waves. He'd done enough of that recently. His agent might kill him if he gave the media another reason to lambast him. "Do you think she'd even want to work for me?"

Chad stood from the table. "I think so. Once she calms down, I think she'll see that this is the best choice."

Skyler tapped the sunglasses in his hand and shook his head at himself. "Do you have a business card? And a pen?"

Chad looked confused but grabbed both out of a pocket inside his suit jacket. He handed the card and pen over to Skyler. Skyler scribbled his cell phone number on the back of the card. He also jotted down a dollar amount—the salary he'd told the recruiter to offer candidates.

"Here." Skyler handed the card and pen back to Chad. "That's my number and an offer for Myra. Tell her to let me know by tomorrow morning if she wants the job. And as long as she's working for me, she can stay in the apartment, rent-free."

Chad glanced down at the card. His eyes briefly widened. "That's a very generous offer. I'll talk with her right now."

Skyler wasn't feeling particularly generous, but he couldn't stop picturing the woman who'd seemed surprised to lose her business and home. He wasn't here to make anyone's life worse. In fact, he was trying to wade through some rough waters himself.

"Make sure she knows I need an answer by the morning." He stepped off the patio and onto the sidewalk. "And Chad?"

"Yes?"

"If that cell phone number ends up in the wrong hands, I'm not going to be very happy."

"Of course." Chad quickly tucked the card in his pocket.

Skyler strode off. The shop was on the edge of the block, and he followed the sidewalk around the corner, got in his car, and immediately started it up. The engine purred to life, and Skyler glanced out the window at the reinvented barn. It really hadn't changed much in decades, at least on the outside.

Reaching over, he popped open the glove box and pulled out a black-and-white photograph—the picture that had led him to Maple Bay. He held it up, looking back and forth between the photograph and real life.

In real life, the barn was apple-red. White trim popped around windows and a double door. The gambrel roof angles framed a metal sign that read *Perkup Coffee*.

In the picture, the building had the same structure, but instead of windows and a double door, a big barn door stood open. A few cows were visible inside. A grassy field surrounded the barn, and there were no houses in sight. But the most interesting piece of the picture was the woman standing in front of the open barn door.

Skyler's grandma posed for the camera. She looked to be maybe twenty years old and full of life. She wore high-waisted capri pants and a collared blouse. A handkerchief was tied in her hair. She pressed one hand against her hip and raised the other in the air. A big smile shone on her face.

Skyler stared at the photograph for a few more seconds. Then he set it on the passenger seat, knowing he'd do anything for the woman in the picture. His grandma was the only person who had always been there for him. This time, he would be there for her.

Chapter Three

Myra spent the rest of the morning in her mother's house, staring at the business card Chad had given her and wondering if she could possibly mess up anything else in her life. She'd single-handedly lost her coffee shop—the business she'd started after Luis and she had divorced. She'd been trying so hard to save it, to catch up on her bills, but one thing after another had kept knocking her down, and she'd fallen so far into this hole that she couldn't see sunlight anymore.

"What have I done?" Myra muttered as she pinched the bridge of her nose, trying to keep from crying again.

When the threat of tears passed, she stood from the kitchen table and walked to the stove. The frying pan had warmed up. Oil was popping, and Myra set the roast in the heat. It sizzled, and she silently savored the distraction before her. She seared all four sides of the roast before grabbing tongs and moving it to the Crockpot. After nestling the seared hunk of meat into a bed of sliced onions, she added chopped garlic and beef broth. Then she set the glass top on the Crockpot, clicked the setting to low, and moved to the sink. However, standing at the sink made it much harder to distract herself from her massive screwup. Out her mother's kitchen window, Myra had a clear view of Perkup. Her mother's flower-filled backyard butted up to the back side of the coffee shop, separated from it only by a gravel alley.

Myra looked down and away from the window. Picking up a potato, she started peeling. She sliced at the brown skin with a ferocity that the potato didn't deserve, but she felt the slightest relief in accomplishing something.

"What am I going to tell my customers?"

Slice, slice, slice.

"What am I going to tell my mom?"

Her slicing sped up. Thin peels launched into the sink.

"What am I going to tell my *kids*?"

Myra's slicing turned into slashing, and when she heard the crunch of gravel outside, her eyes lifted from her task. However, her hands didn't stop moving, and she sliced into her finger as she watched her mom's car pull into the drive at the back of the house.

With a yelp, Myra dropped the potato and the peeler. They bounced into the sink, and blood colored her knuckle.

Myra gave a deep, frustrated sigh before ripping a paper towel from the roll. She wrapped the white sheet around her injured pointer finger and pressed down to stop the bleeding. As she did, the back door opened, and her mother, Judy, appeared. She was talking before she got through the door.

"You know what that cranky doctor told me now? That I'm still supposed to be taking it easy. Doesn't he know I've got stuff to do? Gardens to weed. Grandkids to keep up with. Coffee to pour. If he tells me one more time that I—" Judy's eyes landed on Myra. She stopped her babbling. "What in the heck happened to you?" She closed the door behind her.

I lost the coffee shop.

Myra gave a quick shrug. "Caught my knuckle with the potato peeler."

"Geez, Louise." Judy moved toward Myra. There was a slight hitch in her walk, but she'd been getting around much better since her hip replacement. "You been crying? Your mascara is all over your face." She said it like Myra had forgotten to wear a shirt.

"Oh." Myra's paper towel–bandaged hand went to her face, and she blurted out the first thing she thought of. "No, just got caught in the rain. Those dang spring showers. Caught me off guard when I went to the grocery store this morning."

Judy squinted at Myra. "It rained that hard here? While I was at the clinic?"

"Yeah, just for ten or fifteen minutes, though. It downpoured." It had been a downpour, all right. A downpour of epic proportions.

Satisfied, Judy set her purse on the kitchen table. "Well, good. My garden needed to be watered anyhow. April showers bring May flowers, don't ya know?" Judy peeked through the glass top of the Crockpot. "I'll finish up the roast. You going to help Becca close up?"

"I can finish it, Mom." Myra picked the peeler and potato out of the sink. She gave them both a rinse. "Why don't you sit down and rest?"

"You sound like that cranky doctor." Judy took the peeler from Myra. "Now, hand over the potato and go clean yourself up. You look like you're in worse shape than me."

Myra wasn't sure why she tried to slow her mom down. It never worked. In fact, Judy resisted more when someone told her to relax. The only way to get her mom to take a break was to get a job done *before* Judy found it. Which was why Myra had been attempting to prep supper before Judy got home. Most nights, Myra and the kids had supper with her mom, and she'd been trying to take over all the cooking since Judy's hip had started bothering her late last year. However, Myra often spent more time fighting her mother over cooking duties than she did actually making the meals.

She handed the half-peeled potato to her mom. "Okay. I probably should go help Becca anyhow." It was just after one o'clock, and Becca had been working the shop by herself since Myra had left this morning.

Retreating to the half-bath just off the kitchen, Myra closed the door and looked at herself in the oval mirror.

"Dear Lord, I look like a racoon." Black mascara was smeared under and around her eyes. A dollop of dried smoothie sat on the top of her head like a barrette in her black hair. "A drunk, rabid racoon." *Did I go to the grocery store looking like this?*

She removed the paper towel from her finger and threw it in the trash. At least the peeler wound had stopped bleeding. Then she brushed out the smoothie remnants and redid her ponytail. After wadding up some toilet paper and rubbing her racoon eyes away, Myra thought she'd effectively covered up the evidence of a morning that had gone all wrong. She was presentable. On the outside, anyhow.

Reaching into her jeans pocket, Myra pulled out the business card Chad had given her this morning. He'd said Skyler wanted her to manage the shop. She closed her eyes. Her heart hurt at the thought of it. She'd built her coffee shop from the ground up. After the divorce, she'd used every last dime she had to turn the barn into a business. She'd put sweat, muscle, and countless hours into her coffee shop. She was proud of her creation, but circumstances had allowed it to slip away.

And now, she couldn't believe she was *considering* working for the man that . . . that was the new owner.

Myra leaned against the pedestal sink and stared at the business card in her hand. The salary Skyler had offered was more than double what she'd made in the past year. She'd be stupid to pass it up. She already knew she needed to swallow her pride and take the offer—at least until she figured out what to do next. But that was a hard pill to swallow, so Myra stuffed the card back in her pocket. She had until tomorrow morning to give Skyler an answer.

"I'll be back when the kids get home from school," she said to her mom and left the house. Walking across the alley, Myra forced her chin up. It was quite the feat, because her head felt heavy like a cinderblock. When she stepped into Perkup, Myra saw that Becca had already put the *Closed* sign in the front window. Myra usually closed the shop after lunch, but sometimes kept it open until three—if there were customers.

Today, the dining room was empty. Except for Becca . . . and one man who stood near the register, a briefcase in his hand. Myra didn't recognize him.

Oh, no. Her entire body grew heavy at the thought of having to wade through another conversation about the foreclosure.

"There you are," Becca said from behind the counter. Her short blonde hair brushed against her jaw as she turned toward Myra. "This gentleman was looking for you. Said Skyler sent him." Becca not-so-discreetly shielded her lips with one hand and mouthed, *Who's Skyler?* Her eyes were bright and curious behind her emerald-rimmed glasses.

Before Myra could respond, the man glided toward her. "Myra Wilder?" His dark hair was cut high and tight. A shiny black dress shirt and slacks made him look like he'd just walked out of a wedding. He was way too dressed up for Maple Bay on a Tuesday afternoon.

"Yes?" Myra replied, cringing internally. She didn't want Becca to hear the news about the foreclosure. Becca had been a loyal employee and friend. She was like a little sister and deserved to hear the news from Myra. Not from a stranger. "Hey, Becca. Would you mind running to the market to grab a few cans of whipped cream? I only have one and don't want to run out tomorrow."

"Um, sure," she replied. "Now?"

"Yeah, that'd be great."

"Okay." Becca tilted her head. Myra usually managed the shopping and inventory. "I'll be back in fifteen or so."

"Thanks," Myra said and waited until Becca had gone out the front door. She focused back on the mystery man. "Skyler sent you?"

He offered his hand. Myra shook it. "Cedric Dallon. I'm Skyler's agent, but he doesn't know I'm here."

Myra slid her hand from his. "I thought he said I had until tomorrow to give him an answer." Anxiety coiled in her chest. Was she ready to make a decision? Here and now?

"Are you talking about the job offer?" he asked, and Myra nodded. "Yeah, that's not really why I'm here. I mean, it's kind of why I'm here. But not really."

Myra pinched her eyebrows together. "I'm not following."

"Can we sit?" Cedric motioned to the closest table.

"Sure." She apprehensively took a seat. Cedric sat across the small square table from her. He set his briefcase on the floor, next to his polished leather shoes.

"I'll make this quick," Cedric started. "I've got an offer for you."

"Something different from what Skyler offered?"

"More like something in addition to what he offered," Cedric replied. "Look, Skyler doesn't belong in Maple Bay. I know that, and you know that."

Myra didn't know where Skyler belonged. She didn't care where he belonged. She just wished he hadn't bought her business. "Okay?"

Cedric pushed up the sleeves of his dress shirt like he was getting ready to work. "And I'm sure you've seen all the stories in the press about Skyler in the past week."

Myra nodded. Skyler's face was on every tabloid at the grocery store. His story was flitting around social media, too. She usually didn't pay much attention to that stuff, but had caught the gist of the headlines this morning. They'd been hard to ignore. "That he's been lying to his fans?" she asked. "That he's been feeding fake stories to the press for years. That he's a silver-spooned city boy pretending to be a cowboy."

Cedric made a face like he'd eaten something sour. "Yep. Those stories."

"Is that what he's doing here? Hiding from the press?" She remembered the way Skyler had been dressed this morning—black sunglasses and a low-pulled baseball cap. He'd also shaved off his signature scruffy beard.

"Kind of. Though when you're Skyler Ridge, it's hard to hide anywhere," Cedric said flatly. "After the media got a hold of some leaked information, I told Skyler to lie low while I smoothed over the damage." Myra noticed Cedric didn't say that the tabloids were wrong. "I wanted him to go to some remote island in the Caribbean or hole up at a Four Seasons, but for some reason, he decided to pack up and move to Maple Bay. I tried to talk him out of it, but he was stuck on this place. For the life of me, I don't know why. And now I think he's totally lost his marbles. He's a country music star. Not a coffee shop owner."

"Exactly." Myra crossed her arms over her chest. This whole situation was strange. Certainly, Skyler didn't plan to stay here and sling coffee. "What does he think he's going to do with Perkup?" Myra braced herself for the answer. He'd probably sell it as quickly as he'd bought it. Maybe she could buy it back?

Cedric's face went serious. "Give it to you."

Myra's jaw unhinged, and her mouth fell open. "What do you mean?" She spoke in a tone she thought only dogs could hear.

"I mean, you can have your coffee shop back if you help me get Skyler's music career back on track. After he gets back to singing, he won't have any use for this place."

Her fleeting excitement plummeted. "How am I supposed to save his music career?" Did Cedric have her confused with someone else?

"When Skyler told me he bought this place, I did some research. On the shop. The town. On you."

Myra sat up straight. "What exactly are you asking me to do?"

"You ride horses, right? You go to those rodeo things. You're wearing cowboy boots."

"Uh, yeah." She crossed her legs under the table. The only time she didn't wear boots was when she went barefoot.

"You're a *cowgirl*," Cedric said, like he was announcing a revelation.

She was a cowgirl, and proud of it. "And?"

"And you can make Skyler *look* like a cowboy."

"Didn't he already try that? Hasn't he been lying about having country roots since he set foot in Nashville?" All of Skyler's songs were about dirt roads, cold beer, and big trucks. But the tabloids said Skyler preferred sipping champagne and living the high life in a penthouse. Not a good look for someone that sang hit songs like "Blue-Collared Roots" and "Country to the Core."

Cedric sighed. "I just need you to play along. I'll handle all the details." He shifted forward in his chair. The uneven legs wobbled against the floor. "If you can put Skyler in situations that could redeem his image, I'll make sure pictures are taken and that they get to the press."

"What kind of situations? Like riding a horse into the sunset? Roping a steer? Yelling 'yeehaw'?" She was joking, but Cedric seemed to like what she was saying.

"Yes, yes, and yes." Then, for a second, he paused. "I mean, don't put him in any situation where he's going to look like a fool. Getting him run over by a steer would probably be even worse for his reputation." His face pinched. Myra had no doubt he was imagining a steer stampede.

"You're saying that if I play along with this idea of yours, I can have my coffee shop back?" Her stomach clenched in a silent warning that this crazy offer was too good to be true.

Cedric shifted in his seat. "Skyler's contract with his label is due to be renegotiated in just a few weeks. But if he doesn't fix his image, the label is going to drop him. Then he won't have anything better to do than stick around here and serve coffee."

Myra decided not to take offense to that last part, especially because that was exactly what she was fighting for: the chance to stick around here and serve coffee.

"Honestly, this sounds fishy." She narrowed her eyes at him. "You said Skyler doesn't know you're here? Why?"

"Because he's checked out. He's in a rut. Or at least he thinks he is. He wouldn't agree to this if I asked him, but I know what's best for him. I've been his agent forever. He's just in a bad mental place. He needs to get back to his real life. His music. And you can help him do that."

"And I'm just supposed to trust that Skyler will follow through with his end of *your* deal? That if I do this, he'll actually give me my coffee shop back?"

Cedric dug into his briefcase and pulled out a few papers. He set them on the table and pushed them directly in front of her. "Skyler's lawyer wrote up a legal contract. Read it over and see if it works for you. Feel free to have your legal counsel look over it as well."

Myra pulled the papers close and started reading. The shop was starkly quiet as her eyes moved across legal mumbo jumbo. Essentially, if Myra took part in this plan and Skyler got a new contract with his label, Myra would receive payment in the form of her coffee shop. Perkup would be hers, free and clear. No loans. No mortgage. Just hers.

On the last page of the contract, Skyler's signature was already present.

Myra's gaze slid across the table and met Cedric's waiting stare. His forearms were propped on the edge of the table, his torso tipped forward in anticipation.

"Skyler already signed this?" she asked.

"I can get him to sign anything." He spoke with the confidence of a man who had done this before. "I take care of my clients, and Skyler needs this."

Myra swallowed, not sure she was doing the right thing, but also knowing what this would mean for her and her kids. She could have her livelihood back. Her home. Everything she'd worked for. Besides, Maple Bay was just a pit stop in Skyler Ridge's life. Cedric was right. Skyler didn't belong here.

Myra could help him regain his music career—which would surely bring him enough money to make up for the coffee shop he'd lose. Something he didn't care about. Not like she did.

"I'll do it on one condition," she said. Then she put her boots firmly on the ground and told Cedric what she needed. When he agreed to persuade Skyler of her request, she signed on the dotted line.

Chapter Four

"You don't think she's being awfully demanding?" Skyler asked Cedric, referring to the text he'd received from Myra about an hour ago. "Maybe offering her a job wasn't the best decision." He certainly didn't need another person forcing him into a corner, squeezing him for everything he had. He felt bad for her, but was he letting his heart put him in a bad spot *again*?

"Maybe a little demanding," Cedric replied. "But I think she's just embarrassed. Doesn't want anyone to know she lost the business."

Skyler eyed Cedric over a glass of bourbon. He should've known his agent would come after him. He wasn't one to take no for an answer.

"Maybe." Skyler took a sip. Ice clinked, and oaky warmth coated his throat.

"She obviously cares about that place. You know she'll take good care of it," Cedric replied. "And it's not like you'll live here full time anyhow. You'll need a reliable manager while you're on the road."

The two of them sat, facing each other on the back deck of the house Skyler had bought the same day he'd purchased the coffee shop. The house was on the north side of Maple Leaf Lake, a few miles outside of town, and he couldn't get over how quiet it was here. It was exactly what he needed. *Space. Peace.*

Skyler eased back in the padded patio furniture his assistant had ordered for him. He set socked feet on the footstool. "Who said I'm going back on the road?" Maybe he should buy a boat. Or a couple of jet skis?

Cedric broke into his boat-buying thoughts. "Come on, Sky. You can't just give up your career because of this nonsense in the media. It'll blow over. I'll make sure of it." The sun was setting behind Cedric, sliding into the dark blue waters of the lake. Skyler could get used to such a beautiful view.

"I think I'm just over it," Skyler said, circling the drink in his hand and rattling the ice. He tipped his head back and looked at the dusky evening sky. He was sick of a lot of things—especially being told who he could be and what he could do. "I'm done living out of a hotel, singing songs I don't care about." *Feeling empty.*

"So you're never going to sing again?" Cedric prodded him. He'd been his agent since Skyler had hit it big. Cedric knew how music was ingrained in his soul.

"I've got enough money. Maybe it's time to retire," Skyler half-joked. His ex-wife had taken half his bank account and the house in Los Angeles. He still had more money than he knew what to do with.

"Retire? You just turned forty. You've got a whole career ahead of you. How about you take a vacation instead?" When Skyler didn't reply, Cedric continued pushing. "Take some time to sort out that head of yours. Relax. Do whatever it is that people do around here. I'll handle the media. I'll get this sorted out, and Country Records will be begging you to sign with them for another five years."

Skyler sighed and peeled his stare from the sky. He looked at Cedric, honestly not knowing what he wanted. He was lost and had been for a while.

"What do you think you're going to do with that coffee shop anyhow?" Cedric asked. "You going to get up at the crack of dawn tomorrow and start making lattes? Have someone snap a photo of you in an apron and sell it to the press?"

It was the first thing in quite some time that had made Skyler smirk. "I can only imagine the headlines that would go along with that photo."

"Come on. Don't make this any harder for me. Respond to Myra. Let her handle the coffee shop. You don't need any more stress."

Skyler set his drink on the glass coffee table and picked up his phone. He reread Myra's text from earlier.

Myra: *I'll take the job on one condition. I need you to pretend I still own the place. Will you do that? Pretend to be a silent partner?*

Honestly, Skyler wasn't sure what he was doing anymore. Coming to Maple Bay had been a last-minute decision, something he hoped would shelter him from the storm he was in. But he did know one thing: he was done explaining himself. To *anyone*. At this point, *silent* sounded like a pretty good option.

Skyler typed a response, agreeing to Myra's demand and adding that he'd be by the shop tomorrow to discuss the details. Then he set his phone down and looked back up at the stars.

Skyler's phone rang and jerked him out of sleep. For a few moments, he didn't know where he was. Everything was black. His head was fuzzy. When his brain started to realign, he rolled across the king-sized bed and reached for his phone to silence the irritating ringtone.

What flipping time is it? He snatched the phone off the bedside table and squinted at the glowing screen, determining it was just before five o'clock in the morning. *Myra's calling me? In the middle of the night?*

Reluctantly, he answered the call. "Hello?" It sounded like he'd been gargling gravel.

"Are you still sleeping?" Myra asked, sounding shocked.

Is night a strange time to sleep? "What?"

"Aren't you feeding the horses this morning?"

Definitely had one too many bourbons last night. "Horses?" Skyler squeezed his eyes shut, trying to reset his mind. A minute ago, he'd been sleeping, blissfully unaware of anything to do with horses. "They eat in the middle of the night?"

His question was returned with silence. Then he heard shuffling and a few distinct swear words.

"I don't even know how I did that," Myra finally said into the phone. "Sorry. I meant to call my cousin. It's just that a pipe burst, and I thought he'd be up and could—"

"A pipe burst? In the shop?" His first full day of ownership, and the building was flooding? Skyler shuffled into an upright position. "Where?"

"Under the sink."

"I'll be there in fifteen."

"No, I—" she started, but Skyler hung up and crawled out of bed. Through jumbled thoughts, he found the clothes he'd worn last night. They were still lying on the floor. He jumped into the jeans and threw on the sweatshirt. As he did, he second-guessed his decision to let Myra manage the business. He'd owned Perkup for less than twenty-four hours, and now it was flooding? She was going to call her cousin instead of a plumber? What kind of logic was that? Skyler swore at his own stupidity and ran out to his car.

Myra hadn't paid the bank in months. She'd let her shop and home go into foreclosure. What else had she allowed to fall apart?

I should've told Chad I had the shop handled and left it at that. What have I gotten myself into?

Ten minutes later, Skyler took a sharp turn and parked in front of Perkup. It was still dark out, but the shop was lit up. He jumped out of his car and jogged to the door. A bell jingled over his head as he stepped inside, expecting to be met with a lake of water.

The floor was dry. The shop was empty. No one was in sight.

"Back here," Myra called from somewhere behind the counter.

Skyler followed her voice and slid around the edge of the counter. "I called the only plumber I could find," he replied, still looking for a gushing pipe. Instead, he found Myra. She was lying on her back, half concealed under the sink. Five or six wet towels were scattered about. A few puddles were visible on the wood floor, but it wasn't the disaster he'd imagined.

Myra scooted out from under the sink, showing her face. She didn't look nearly as distressed as he was. "You called Bob? Why?"

"Because we need a plumber." Bob's Plumbing was the first number that had popped up on his phone when he'd Googled plumbers in Maple Bay. Seemed like a rational decision. "Got his voicemail, but I left a message." He pulled his phone from his pocket and looked at the screen. "He hasn't called back yet."

"He won't. Not for a few hours. Bob doesn't get up before seven o'clock unless it's deer season. And it's definitely not deer season."

"What?" Why were they talking about deer season? And was there only one plumber in this whole town? "I thought you said a pipe burst."

"It did. Let loose when I came down this morning to start the coffee." Myra shimmied out from under the sink and sat up. She draped an arm around a bent leg. A wrench glinted in her hand. "I was hoping to get it fixed before the morning rush but will have to wait for my cousin to get here. He's bringing the parts I need." She grabbed a silver pipe from inside the cabinet, stood, and placed the pipe and wrench on the counter.

Skyler suddenly had to resist the urge to dig through his wallet for his man card. He had a phone in his hand. Myra had a wrench. "You're going to fix it?"

She looked at him hesitantly. "Yeah. It's pretty simple. I'll put the new pipe in once Jesse gets here. That's my cousin. The person I *meant* to call this morning. I honestly didn't mean to wake you up. Sorry about that. I've got this handled. You can go back to bed." Myra gave him a once-over, and he suddenly realized he hadn't looked in a mirror before he'd rushed out of his house. Myra looked fresh as a daisy. Her black hair was pulled into a neat braid that hung down her back. Her blue eyes were bright. She wasn't even wet. How'd she managed that?

Skyler scraped a hand through his hair. It felt like he had a major case of bedhead. "I thought there was an emergency." He'd sped here like he was on a racetrack. The whole time, he'd cursed Myra's name, thinking she had no business managing his shop.

"I would've told you I had it handled if you'd have let me talk," Myra said. One eyebrow arched in judgement. "You hung up before I could."

Skyler was at a loss for words, and that rarely happened. Myra's disdain for him was apparent—in her tone and body language. She did *not* like him, and there was no way this was going to work. It didn't matter if she could handle the shop or not. She couldn't handle *him*. He felt like he was flying down the highway and had to choose whether or not to get off at the next exit.

"Look, I don't know if this is going to work," Skyler started, not wanting another obstacle in his life. Myra jerked her gaze to him. "I know I agreed to it last night, but I think it'd be best if we just parted ways. You can stay upstairs as long as it takes to find a new place, but—"

"Momma!" A child's voice rang out, silencing Skyler. For a brief second, Skyler thought he saw fear in Myra's face. It vanished as soon as her son tromped in from the back hall. "I got more towels from Grandma!" The same little boy Skyler had seen yesterday ran into the shop, carrying a stack of towels that went up to his chin. He ran to Myra, and she took the cloths from him.

"Finchy," Myra said, setting the towels next to the sink. "This is Mr. Ridge. Can you introduce yourself?"

"Oh, yeah. The smoothie guy. I remember." The little boy smiled. He had dark hair, the same shade as his mom's. The hems of his truck-themed pajamas hovered above a pair of cowboy boots. "Hi, Mr. Ridge. I'm Finch Wilder. Momma said you play a guitar. So cool!" He reached out his hand. "You can call me Finchy, like everyone else does."

"Nice to meet you, Finchy." Skyler shook the boy's hand. "You can call me Skyler. Or Sky." He wasn't used to anyone calling him Mister.

"Okay, Sky." Finch let go of his hand and tugged his pajama pants up on his belly. They'd been slipping down while he carried the towels. "Momma also said you're going to help us."

Skyler froze. Myra turned away, immediately busying herself by grabbing a dry towel and handing it to Finch. "Let's get this water cleaned up so I can get you some breakfast."

Finch took the cloth but seemed oblivious to his mom's discomfort. "That's awesome," Finch said to Skyler. "Do you know how to make coffee?"

His question was so innocent. Skyler wondered what exactly Myra had told her son. "Um, yeah. I can make coffee."

Finch got down on the floor and tossed a towel over a puddle near the base of the fridge. "Mom won't let me have any coffee yet, but I can make it." He sounded proud.

A door opened, and more footfalls came from the back hall. Myra's teenage daughter appeared. She was also in pajamas—an oversized T-shirt with a horse print on it that read *Unstable Before Noon*. Her hair spilled over her shoulders. She wore glasses and was carrying a bucket and mop. When she saw Skyler, she went stick-straight and screamed. Dropping the bucket and mop, she ran back into the hall, narrowly avoiding an older woman.

"Goodness," the woman said, but understanding hit her face when she saw Skyler. "Oh, we weren't expecting company. Glad I changed out of *my* pajamas before coming over." She laughed and entered the shop, carrying two jugs of water. Myra walked over and took the jugs from her.

"Thanks, Mom." Myra set the containers next to the coffee maker. "That'll work until we can turn the water back on."

"I'm Judy. Myra's mom." Judy walked toward Skyler with a bit of a limp. She reached out, and Skyler stepped forward to meet her. Instead of shaking his hand, she grasped it with both of hers, making a hand sandwich. "Myra told me all about you. We are so grateful that you decided to invest in our little coffee shop. We're so excited to have you as a partner."

Skyler caught Myra's eye over Judy's shoulder. She was pouring water into the top of a coffee maker. Her lips were pressed tightly together, but all the disdain had leaked out of her and dripped into the puddle still at her feet.

"Mom, I need to tell you something." Myra set the jug down and closed the coffee maker. She braced herself on the edge of the counter. Her head drooped. Judy looked confused, and Skyler's stomach twisted. It wasn't like he hadn't put himself in a few tight spots, taken the wrong path even when the right one had been laid out before him. He might regret it, but something inside was urging him to give Myra a little grace and more than a day to prove herself.

Skyler cleared his throat. "Hey, Finch?" he asked. "Can you give me one of those towels?"

Finch jumped up from the floor and delivered a towel.

"Thanks." Skyler gave Finch a smile. "We better get this place cleaned up so we can open, right?"

Finch nodded enthusiastically.

Skyler turned to Judy. "I'm excited for this partnership as well." He smiled, and Judy seemed to forget all about Myra's comment.

Still standing next to the coffee maker, Myra looked stunned. Especially when Skyler got on all fours and started wiping up the floor. Though he wished he had a towel big enough to clean up the rest of his life.

Chapter Five

"Finchy, can you take all of the towels upstairs and put them by the washing machine?" Myra asked as she pressed *Start* on both coffee makers. The rising sun peeked through the shop windows. Customers would be arriving shortly.

Finch popped up from the floor. He and Skyler had just finished wiping up the last of the water on the floor. "Then can I help pour coffee?"

"After you take a shower and get dressed for school."

Finch made a face like he didn't understand the need for cleanliness. "Okay." He gathered the wet towels. "I'll be back!" He ran off toward the back hall and bounced up the stairs with a series of thumps.

Skyler stood from his crouched position on the floor. "I wish I had as much energy as your son does."

Myra glanced at him, still not believing Mr. Country Music Star had gotten on his hands and knees and mopped the floor. Or that he hadn't called her out in front of her mom.

"I find myself wishing that often," Myra replied. Her son was like the Energizer Bunny.

"Sweet kid."

"Thanks." Myra swallowed hard, pushing down her pride. "I'm sorry. I know I'm being bullheaded. This is just a lot for me to take in. I do really appreciate everything you're doing."

Offering her a job and a roof over her head. Playing along with her request to keep his purchase a secret. No matter what Myra thought of Skyler, he currently held all the cards. If she didn't adjust her attitude, she would fall further into a hole. Skyler had confirmed that risk this morning with a swift kick to her ego—letting her know his offer could disappear in an instant.

"Can we start fresh?" Myra closed the space between them and offered her hand. An olive branch. Kind of.

Skyler hesitated but then shook it. "Sure." His grip was strong, his palm still wet from the towels.

Just then, the front door opened. The bell jingled, and Myra's cousin Jesse entered the shop.

"Pipe and scone delivery," Jesse announced, and Myra let her hand fall from Skyler's.

She turned toward Jesse. He was carrying a Tupperware container. A silver pipe lay on top of it. "You are *the best*. Thank you so much."

Jesse offered the container, reaching over the counter. Myra took it from him.

"Would've been here earlier, but the scones weren't quite done," Jesse said. Under the brim of his cowboy hat, his gaze wandered over to inspect Skyler. Myra wondered if Jesse recognized him. She hadn't at first glance. The lack of scruffy beard had thrown her off. "Hazel made a batch of cranberry-orange scones."

"She did?" Myra's stomach rumbled at the mention of Hazel's baked goods. "Must be feeling better today, then?"

"Yeah, thankfully. She was up early and insisted on baking." Jesse gave Myra a quizzical look, asking her with his eyes if she was going to introduce the stranger behind her.

"Jesse, this is Skyler." Myra took the container of baked goods and moved toward the empty glass case on the other side of the register. The two men shook hands.

"The investor, right? From Nashville?" Jesse asked. "Mom told me about you. Nice to meet you."

Myra cringed as she situated the scones in the glass case, wondering if her mom had also spilled the beans about exactly *who* Skyler was. Last night, after Skyler had responded to her text, Myra had told her mom about the "silent partner." She had also asked Judy to keep his identity to herself, for now. Eventually, the news would get out, but Myra didn't want to fan the fire of small-town gossip. But Judy must've said something to her sister Joyce, who was Jesse's mom.

"That's me. The investor," Skyler replied after an awkward beat. "Nice to meet you as well."

Myra immediately changed the subject. "Jesse's wife, Hazel, is pregnant. Eight months along. She's an amazing baker and usually makes all the pastries for the shop, but the poor thing's been nauseated for most of her pregnancy and hasn't been able to be on her feet much."

"Which is absolutely driving her crazy," Jesse added, seemingly distracted by the new topic of discussion. "Hazel loves to bake. And she feels so bad she can't help you out."

Myra closed the glass case, which was now filled with scones. "I told her not to worry about me. I just want her to feel better." With Hazel down and out, Myra had been stocking the pastry case with bagels and muffins from the grocery store. It wasn't the best option, but it was the easiest. She didn't have time to bake sweet treats. She barely had time to sleep. "Everyone will be so excited to see her scones this morning. Tell her thank you from me and that I'll stop by after I feed the horses tonight." She handed the empty container back to Jesse.

"Will do," Jesse said. "I'll see you later, then. I've got to get over to Elmwood this morning. Got a few colts to get started under saddle at Mary Wilson's barn."

"Tell Mary I said hello." Myra waved. "And thanks again. You're a lifesaver."

"No problem." Jesse turned toward the door. Over his shoulder he said, "Welcome to Maple Bay, Skyler. I'm sure I'll see you around."

"Thanks," Skyler replied as Jesse headed out the door.

Myra turned to Skyler and immediately addressed the awkward-
ness. "You might've been better off hiding in a big city. News
travels fast in this town. I told my mom not to tell anyone, but—"

"Who said I was hiding?" Skyler asked, putting a stop to Myra
running her mouth. She suddenly realized he hadn't told her that.
It was Cedric who had said Skyler needed to lie low.

"Oh, I guess I just assumed that's why you moved here. What
with the stuff in the news and all."

Skyler cocked his head. His forehead wrinkled. "I mean, I did
want to get away from the media for a bit. But I'm not hiding."

"Okay." Myra grabbed the pipe off the counter, looking for an
immediate escape. "Better get this fixed." She crouched down and
crawled into the open cabinet under the sink. Would it be weird if
she fully crawled inside and shut the door?

"You need any help?" Skyler asked as she tightened the couplers,
putting the new pipe in place.

"Nah, I got this," Myra replied. Besides, if her hands were busy,
her mouth was less likely to get her in trouble.

The rest of the day flew by, punctuated by texts from Cedric. He
had a photographer on standby, ready to snap pictures of Skyler
at a moment's notice. Myra just needed to tell Cedric when and
where, and the photographer would get there.

After cleaning up the shop and devising a half-baked plan, Myra decided it was time to follow through. She took her apron off and hung it by the espresso machine. Then she took a big breath and walked down the hallway to her office. *His office. Our office. Whatever.*

She poked her head in the office, which wasn't much bigger than the pastry case out front. She could close the door easily from her seat at the desk.

"Find anything interesting?" Myra asked.

Skyler was sitting at the desk. He looked up from a thick binder filled with records, invoices, and financials. "I haven't made much of a dent in the file cabinet yet."

"Let me know if you have questions," she offered.

This morning, Skyler had taken off after the pipe was fixed but had come back after lunch. He'd been holed up in the office since. She was surprised he was going through the files himself. Myra had assumed he'd hire an accountant, assistant, or some fancy consultant. Someone that would gobble up the information and spit out a packaged response on how to increase sales by five million percent. *Get a Facebook page. Start tweeting about coffee. You need a rewards program.* She could hear the brilliant ideas now.

"I will," he replied and looked back at the papers. Myra followed his gaze—and saw an excuse to get Skyler in her truck.

She pointed at the invoice he was scanning. A bill from Northern Coffee Roasters. "I was just going to make a run over to Northern Roasters. I need to drop off a check for next week's delivery. Or, I guess *you* need to write a check for next week's delivery." The words felt funny coming out of her mouth. Like she was passing off her responsibilities or asking for a handout. But this wasn't her business anymore . . . not for now. "It's just outside of town, and you could meet Gabriel. He's the roaster. I'm sure he could give you a tour of the facility."

Skyler looked at the clock on the wall like he had somewhere to be, but Myra knew the rest of his day was free. Cedric had told her so.

"I think I'm just going to stay here," he said. "Can I call him with a credit card number to pay the bill?" Skyler thumbed to the next page in the binder, his brow furrowed.

Skyler had bought a coffee shop but wasn't interested in the product he was selling? Myra pressed her lips together, thinking. "Gabriel doesn't take credit cards," she replied, and it wasn't a lie. "Cash or check." The eighty-year-old man didn't trust plastic.

Skyler gave her a puzzled stare. "Really?"

"Really. Come on. It won't take long. Don't you want to meet the man that's responsible for the coffee you sell?"

Skyler tapped a pen against the desk. "I guess. If it'll be quick."

"Great. I'll drive. I'm parked out back." She stepped away before Skyler could come up with a reason not to go. "See you out there."

A few minutes later, Skyler waltzed out the back door and toward the alley, where Myra sat in her truck. As he opened the passenger door, Myra hit *Send* on a text to Cedric, giving him the address of her aunt and uncle's house.

Skyler climbed in and slid onto the bench seat. "This truck is huge."

Myra started the vehicle, thinking his comment odd. "What'd you expect me to drive? A Volkswagen Beetle?"

"No, this makes sense." He gave a dry chuckle that rubbed her the wrong way.

As Skyler put his seat belt on, Myra narrowed her eyes at him, digesting his comment. She drove a big, old Ford dually with a diesel engine that would probably outlive the truck's mustard-yellow paint. Her truck was steady, strong, and rarely gave her flak. It was exactly what she needed. Come to think of it, Skyler's car made sense for him too. His sporty little Mercedes fit him to a tee. Flashy and out of place in Maple Bay.

But she kept that comment to herself.

Chapter Six

After a full tour of Northern Coffee Roasters, Skyler was back in Myra's truck watching the countryside whip by out an open window. Yesterday's rain had vanished. Sun warmed his forearm where it rested on the door, and the cab was filled with the sound of whooshing wind. His gaze settled on Myra. She drove with one hand on the steering wheel, looking like it was no big deal to drive a vehicle one step below a semi-truck. He couldn't picture his ex-wife handling something like this. Cassidy hadn't even liked driving the Mercedes she'd insisted they buy. She liked being seen in it and making a show of it, but she wasn't a fan of driving. She'd rather be chauffeured around. And she'd easily given up the car in the divorce. It was one of the few things she hadn't fought tooth and nail for. The car and their relationship: the two things she'd left in the dust.

Myra gave him a quick glance. Strands of dark hair whipped around her face from where they'd come loose from her braid. "Do you mind if we make a quick stop?"

"Stop? Where?" Northern Coffee Roasters was maybe fifteen minutes outside of Maple Bay. Other than farmland, he hadn't noticed much on the drive over. "I'm not really sure I have time." He wanted to get back to Perkup and continue sifting through files. He wondered if there were any details on the previous owners. Any insight that might link his grandma to the building or the town. He was also hoping to understand how Myra had fallen so far in the red. Though with Myra's sporadic record keeping, he wasn't sure he'd get the full story.

Myra didn't acknowledge his lack of time. She slowed down and turned into a driveway.

"My aunt and uncle's place," she noted. "It'll only take a few minutes. I promise. I totally forgot I picked up some Bute from the vet yesterday." She nodded toward a white canister on the floor. "It's like horse aspirin. One of the mares came up lame this week and needs it."

"Okay." Skyler shrugged. The truck was already halfway down the gravel drive. Apparently, he was along for the ride, whether he liked it or not.

The driveway wound past a cherry-red farmhouse with white shutters. Blooming flowers edged the house, which looked like it had been ripped straight from the pages of a storybook. Behind the house, fenced fields surrounded a wide red barn.

Myra pulled up to the front of the barn and parked. A white horse whinnied from the closest field as soon as she killed the engine.

"There's my Prince Charming," Myra cooed out the window with a sweetness that would've knocked Skyler over if he'd been standing. In the past twenty-four hours, he wasn't sure he'd seen her do anything other than grimace and scowl.

"Your horse?" he asked.

"Yes." Myra turned back toward Skyler. He caught the end of a bright smile that had been aimed at her horse.

"Prince Charming?"

"Charm, for short. My daughter named him, but it suits him. He's the only Prince Charming I have room for in my life."

Skyler chuckled at her unexpected comment. "Handsome horse."

Myra's phone buzzed, and she grabbed it out of the middle console. It had been buzzing nonstop since they'd left the shop. "Do you want to meet Charm?"

Her question took Skyler aback. Until that very second, Myra had been nothing but cold to him. *An ice princess . . . No, an ice queen.* The sudden thawing unnerved him. "I . . . uh. To be honest, I'm not that great with horses."

"Oh." Myra scrunched up her nose. "Aren't you on a horse in most of your music videos?"

He grimaced, not wanting to tackle this topic. But with what the media was saying about him, what did it matter?

"Stunt double," he admitted. Skyler had been on a few horses early on in his career, but something bad always happened when he was in the saddle. After the last horse had tried to rub him off on a tree, Skyler had requested stunt doubles for all riding scenes. "I don't mix well with large animals."

Myra glared at him like he was a monster. Her phone buzzed in her hand and knocked her out of her judgmental stare. "Okay . . . well . . . I . . ." She snatched the white container from the floorboard. "I'm going to give that mare some Bute. Do you want to come in? See the barn?"

Skyler shook his head. "Uh . . . no, thanks. I'll just wait here."

"Yeah. Sure. Cool." She tucked a loose strand of hair behind her ear.

What was happening? Was she nervous? Was the horse she needed to medicate some monster that might eat her alive? Did she think he could help her? Before he could ask what was going on, Myra hoisted herself out of the truck. She walked into the barn and, through the open door, Skyler saw her move down the long alleyway lined with horse stalls. A few horses poked their heads out of the stalls as she walked by. Skyler watched curiously as Myra zipped back and forth across the hall a few times and then disappeared.

"Huh," he said to himself before sitting back and dismissing the odd behavior. He pulled his phone from his jeans pocket, looking for something to do while he waited, but there wasn't much to distract him. Unlike Myra's phone, his had been silent most of the day. It helped that he'd stripped it clean of most apps. *No social media. No newsfeed.* Basically, he could call, text, and check the weather.

The other week, when Cassidy had sold him out to the media, his phone had exploded with rings and dings. Every entertainment channel and tabloid had slashed his name to bits and pieces. Cedric was frantic. The label was furious. And every time his phone made a noise, Skyler saw his music career slipping further and further into a hole. A deep, dark hole. It would probably settle in the depths, next to his sham of a marriage.

But regardless of what Cassidy did, Skyler knew he'd put himself in this spot. He'd gotten lost in the glitz and glamour of the spotlight. Sold his own soul in exchange for a record deal. And now he was paying the consequences. Skyler rubbed the back of his neck, trying to forget the fiasco. As he did, his phone rang, reminding Skyler that he'd never escape.

When he saw the name on the screen, his stomach dropped. He immediately picked up.

"Hey, Carol. Everything okay?"

"I—uh," she started. "Dorthea is gone."

Skyler's insides did a flip-flop. He sat up ramrod straight. "What do you mean?"

"I went to go make tea, and now she's gone. She's not in her bedroom. I've searched the whole house. I don't know where she is." The panic in Carol's voice sent Skyler reeling.

"You were only gone a few minutes?"

"Yes."

"Keep looking. I'm just outside of town. I'm coming." Skyler was out of the truck before he ended the call.

Chapter Seven

"You didn't tell me he was afraid of horses," Myra said into her phone. She stood in the tack room, surrounded by leather, not knowing how she was supposed to make Skyler look like a cowboy if he wouldn't go near a horse. "That makes this a *little* trickier."

"Just get him out of the truck and relatively close to a horse," Cedric replied, like that was a simple feat. "Or even next to the barn. The photographer said she's got him in her sight, but all she's got is a few pictures of him in your truck."

How would she accomplish that? Before signing up for this, she should've considered how bad of a liar she was. Her thoughts tended to roll off her tongue faster than her brain could stop them—which had gotten her into hot water more times than she could count. She couldn't even lie when she should.

Myra pinched the bridge of her nose, mulling over her options. Could she play a damsel in distress? Pretend she tweaked her back and ask Skyler to carry a hay bale or lead a horse? *Oh, boy.* She'd need to dig deep to play that card. Did she have those kinds of acting chops?

"Tell the photographer I'll have him out by the horses in five minutes. I just need to—" She paused, hearing her name as it was shouted through the barn. The yell was loud enough to bounce off the rafters. *Was that Skyler?* "Gotta go." She hung up the phone and stuffed it in her pocket.

"Myra!" the shout came again.

She scrambled out of the tack room. "Yes?" Skyler was jogging down the aisle, and he pulled up short when he spotted her.

"Come on." He waved impatiently. "We've got to go. *Now.*"

"Wait. What?" From the way he'd yelled her name, she'd thought there was an emergency. Was he just tired of waiting for her? "I'm not ready to go yet. I've got to—"

"Then give me your keys," he said abruptly. He stuck his hand out like he expected her to hand them over immediately. She was about to tell him to check his demanding celebrity ego, but the look on his face stopped her. Something was wrong.

"What happened?" she asked.

"It's my grandma. Her nurse just called. She can't find her."

"Your grandma?" Did he need to get to the airport?

Skyler took Myra by the elbow and tugged her.

The irritation fizzled out of her. She started walking with him. "Her nurse lost her?"

Skyler's face crumpled for a moment. "My grandma has dementia and she . . . she doesn't know this place. I need to get to my house."

His grandma lived with him? Myra started jogging alongside Skyler. He let go of her arm.

"Okay," she said. "Tell me where to go, and I'll get us there."

They raced to the truck and drove back up the drive. As they did, Skyler gave her directions. Myra mentally followed his list of turns.

"You bought the Churches' place?" she asked, knowing this area like the back of her hand. She'd never been inside the Churches' house but knew exactly where it was. The sprawling log cabin could be seen from a boat on the lake. Mr. Church was the only lawyer in town, but he'd retired a few years ago, leaving the practice to his son. He and his wife had moved to Florida at least a year ago, and their house had sat on the market since. It was a little pricey for this area.

"You know where it is?" Skyler asked.

"Yeah." She turned out of the drive, asking her diesel engine to go. It roared in response. "And I know a faster way to get there."

Dust billowed in the rearview mirror as Myra navigated a few gravel roads winding along corn fields. Skyler was quiet as she drove, and when she pulled onto the road that ran along the north side of the lake, she glanced at him. He was leaning forward, his hand on the dash, his forearm tight. If he could've pushed the truck forward with his body, he would've.

"She'll be okay." Myra felt a need to reassure him, even though she didn't know exactly what was going on.

"I shouldn't have left her," Skyler mumbled, almost to himself. His eyes were on the road, but also far off.

"How long has she been gone?"

"Not long. Carol said she just stepped away to make tea and then couldn't find her."

Myra turned onto the one-lane road that led to the Churches' old house. Tall oak trees created dense cover on both sides of the street. The log cabin was the only house on the dead-end road.

"She couldn't have gone far. We'll find her," Myra said, now thinking of her own grandpa. He was in his eighties, but sharp as a whip and still lived on his own. He came into the shop for coffee every morning. Played poker with his friends every Thursday night. He still drove. She didn't want to picture what it would look like if he suddenly couldn't remember where he was.

As they pulled up to the large log cabin, Skyler said, "Her name is Dorthea. She's tiny. Maybe a hundred pounds. Short, white hair. And she has a brace on her arm." Myra parked the truck and looked at Skyler. "She fell and broke her wrist the last time she wandered off on her own."

There was guilt in his admission, and Myra wasn't sure what to say. Just then, a woman raced around the side of the house. She looked to be in her fifties—not Skyler's grandma. Myra assumed this was Carol, the nurse. Skyler and Myra jumped out of the truck and met her at the front of the house.

"I'm so sorry," Carol said, looking like she was about in tears.

"It's okay." Skyler put his hand on her arm, calming Carol even though he was obviously worried. "You checked everywhere in the house?"

"Yes. Everywhere. I just came outside to look. Do you want me to call the police?"

"I don't want to scare her," Skyler said. "Let's separate and check the area first, okay? Can you stay close to the house? Myra and I will start walking the property."

"Okay." Carol nodded, pressing her lips tightly together.

"I'll go left. You go right?" Myra asked.

Skyler gave a sharp nod. "You have your cell?"

Myra touched her back jeans pocket, feeling the bulge of her phone. It was exactly where she'd stuffed it after ending her call with Cedric. The reminder soured her stomach. "Yeah."

"Call me if you find her."

They parted ways. Myra jogged around the house and through the backyard, which faded into rocks, sand, and the shoreline. Her eyes darted around. Dorthea wouldn't have wandered into the woods, would she? The forest around Skyler's house was dense with fallen branches and brush. It wouldn't be a good place for a stroll. Maybe she'd walked the shoreline? Myra followed the edge of the lake, looking for footprints, but this part of the lake was more rocky than sandy. Cattails and marshy grass jutted out into the shallows. If Dorthea was out here, Myra certainly hoped she hadn't slipped and fallen. It wouldn't be a soft landing. Furthermore, she could've ended up in the water.

But as Myra made her way past a gnarled oak tree, she laid her eyes on a woman who had to be Skyler's grandma. The elderly lady was sitting on a fallen tree trunk, gazing out over the lake. A slight breeze tousled her snow-white hair. Her hands rested in her lap. Myra noticed the black brace around one wrist.

She immediately pulled out her phone and called Skyler. He picked up in one ring.

"You find her?" he asked.

"Yes. Follow the shore to the left of your house. She's okay. Sitting and watching the lake."

There was a relieved sigh from Skyler, but when he hung up, Myra wasn't sure what to do until he arrived. Myra didn't want to upset Dorthea—especially because Dorthea didn't know her. It was probably best to wait for Skyler before approaching. Besides, Dorthea was safe. Actually, she looked happy.

Just then, a duck landed on the water. It squawked, and Dorthea turned her head, following the bird. She saw Myra.

Dorthea's face went from serene to confused.

Myra stepped toward her. "Hi, Dorthea. I'm Myra. I'm a friend of Skyler's. He'll be here in just a minute."

Recognition captured Dorthea's wrinkles. "Oh, sweetie. Come here. Come sit with me. You must see the babies." She spoke like she knew who Myra was, and Myra didn't correct her. She knew enough about dementia to understand it was better to play along with whatever reality consumed Dorthea.

As Myra walked closer, Dorthea smiled. Myra returned her smile and took a seat next to Dorthea on the fallen tree.

"Do you see them?" Dorthea pointed with the arm bound by the brace. Myra followed her gesture. In the cattails, a female wood duck paddled alongside four fuzzy ducklings.

"Oh," Myra replied. "Yes. Baby *ducks*."

"Aren't they adorable?"

"They sure are."

"You know, this is the time of year the mommas push their babies out of their nests," Dorthea said. "This may be their first time in the water."

"I bet it is," Myra replied, and they watched the ducklings glide in a line behind their brown-feathered mother. They moved through tall cattails.

"Spring is my favorite time of year." Dorthea's gaze stayed with the ducklings. "Everything fresh and blooming. My roses should be budding soon, you know."

"Roses are my favorite flower," Myra said just as she heard the crunch of footfalls behind her. She turned. Skyler was jogging along the shore, jaw tense and eyes already scanning his grandmother for signs of injury.

"Grandma." He walked over, looking like he'd just released all the air from his lungs with that one word.

"Sky," Dorthea replied, cheer in her voice. "Come. Join us. See the babies."

"The baby ducks," Myra reiterated when she saw worry on Skyler's face. Then she gave Skyler a smile, trying to tell him he could relax now. His grandma was fine.

Skyler joined them on the tree, sitting on the opposite side of his grandma. He looked out over the lake, though Myra wasn't sure he was watching the wildlife. They sat there for another few minutes, listening to Dorthea coo over the fuzzy ducklings before she gave a cough.

"Grandma, let's get you back inside," Skyler said, concern back on his face. "You're still recovering from that nasty cold. I don't want you to get chilled." Dorthea was wearing a light sweater, and it was barely fifty degrees outside. She probably was cold.

Dorthea gave Skyler a wave of her hand. "You worry too much about me. I'm just fine."

"But Carol made you some tea. Doesn't that sound good?" he asked.

They sat in silence, and Myra thought Dorthea was going to brush her grandson off again, but then Dorthea asked, "What kind of tea did she make?" Her question sounded innocent and offhanded, like she wasn't quite ready to give in to Skyler's request.

"Your favorite. Peppermint."

Dorthea's thin, white eyebrows rose. "Well, that does sound pretty tasty."

Skyler rose and offered his hand. "Let's go have some tea."

Dorthea put her hand in his. Then she turned to Myra. "Will you join us?" A twinkle showed in her hazel eyes. They had the same copper flecks as Skyler's.

"I'd love to." Myra rose from her seat. Dorthea followed.

By the time the three of them made it back to the house, Myra saw that the excursion had worn Dorthea out, even though she didn't want to admit it. Carol met them at the back door, fussing over Dorthea but not making a big deal about her disappearance.

Skyler opened a set of French doors, and they all walked into the kitchen. Granite counters sparkled in the sunlight. Knotty oak cabinets blended perfectly with rustic log-cabin walls. A chandelier made of faux candles hung above a huge butcher-block island. It was one of the prettiest kitchens Myra had ever seen.

"I might lie down for just a few minutes," Dorthea said quietly.

"A little nap never hurt anybody," Skyler replied. "Let's get you settled, and I'll bring you your tea."

"Tea?" Dorthea asked. "You're such a sweet boy." She patted him on the arm.

Skyler gently put his arm around her shoulders. He gave her a kiss on her temple and led her out of the kitchen. Carol joined them, and as they disappeared, Myra couldn't get over how different Skyler was around his grandma. Not that Myra knew him well, but Skyler Ridge, the singer, was the wild boy of country music. He'd dated every pretty face in Hollywood. He partied hard, and there were plenty of pictures to prove it. Myra had seen them plastered all over the tabloid covers at the grocery store. He wasn't the kind of guy that kissed his grandma on the temple and got her tea. *Is he?*

Myra blinked, still staring at the hallway as Carol reappeared. She gave Myra a soft smile and shuffled toward the stove.

"Can I do anything to help?" Myra asked, feeling out of place.

"Oh, no. I just came to get Dorthea her tea." Carol took the teapot off the stove and filled a mug. As she did, Myra heard the strumming of a guitar coming from somewhere down the hallway. A deep male voice joined the guitar. Myra froze in disbelief.

Carol picked the steaming mug up off the counter. She smiled. "She loves it when he sings to her." Then Carol scuttled off into the hallway, leaving Myra by herself, eavesdropping on the warm tones of Skyler's voice. He was singing an old country song. A love song. *Soft and sweet.* It was completely opposite of the country rock that Skyler Ridge was known for. *Is he singing a lullaby for his grandma?*

Myra's heart clenched. Questions bounced through her head. Who was this man? Because *this* man did not line up with who she'd thought Skyler was.

Chapter Eight

Skyler propped his guitar in the corner of the bedroom, careful not to make too much noise. His grandma was peacefully sleeping, giving soft snores, which put him at ease. Today had been hard. He was hoping there'd be fewer hard days now that they were in Maple Bay, but Dorthea was in a house she didn't know. What had he expected? Dorthea did better in environments she recognized, which was why he'd surrounded her with familiar objects. The quilt she'd made years ago with her sisters. The lamp with the colorful stained-glass shade that Grandpa had given her for their fiftieth anniversary. The watercolor painting of the house she'd shared with Grandpa for most of those fifty years—the same home Skyler had moved her out of a few years after Grandpa had passed, when her memory had started slipping . . . after she'd left the oven on and nearly burned the house down while she was sleeping.

Everything he did—for her, at least—he did out of love, but not all decisions were easy. Even if they were in her best interests. He only hoped he'd made a good decision in moving her to Maple Bay. He hoped the memories she'd made here would come back to her, make her happy. He also wanted her far away from the paparazzi in Nashville. If they'd continued to live there, Skyler would've only brought more chaos into his grandma's life. Especially with how the media had started hounding him when the truth had gotten out. Or part of the truth, anyway.

Stepping to her bedside, Skyler tucked the quilt around her shoulders. "Sweet dreams," he whispered. Then he closed the bedroom door and walked down the hall, the same worries hanging heavily on his shoulders. When he stepped into the kitchen, he found Myra perched on a stool at the island. She looked over at him like he was the last man she'd expected to see.

The stool squeaked as she swiveled toward him. "That was beautiful." Her soft words didn't match her surprised face. Skyler wasn't sure what to make of it.

"Thanks," he replied, feeling exposed, knowing she'd heard him sing even if it was from behind a closed door. He was used to performing for huge crowds of screaming fans, but singing for his grandma was always a private show. This was not an area of his life he let many people into. And he'd let Myra in on accident. "The music helps her sleep." It also helped her remember, which was why he sang the same handful of songs, over and over.

Myra nodded and then glanced down at two steaming mugs on the island. She gently pushed one toward him. "I poured you some tea. Wasn't sure how you took it."

Stepping to the edge of the island, he grasped the mug. "Just like this. Thank you." He let the mug warm his hand before taking a sip.

Myra did the same. The house was so quiet that he heard her swallow.

"My grandma had dementia as well," Myra said, breaking the silence. She curled both hands around her mug and pulled it close to her chest. "She passed about ten years ago, but I remember how hard it was to watch her lose her memories and struggle. I'm sorry you and Dorthea are going through this right now." Her gaze was soft. Steady. *Gentle*. It was drastically different from how she'd been side-eying him since they met.

Skyler took another sip of the peppermint tea, focusing on the warmth as it coated his throat. Usually, he would never talk about his grandma to a stranger. He barely knew Myra, but she had just dropped everything to help him find Dorthea, to make sure she was safe. Then she'd sat with his grandma and talked about ducklings.

He set the mug down, deciding to let her in. A little bit. "Some days are worse than others."

Myra took a breath, her chest moving up and down, and Skyler thought he felt his own chest ease. He hadn't really confided in anyone about how tough it had been to watch his grandma's memory slip. He wasn't even sure if he'd handled today's crisis the right way. He had no one else to ask—other than professionals.

"How long?" Myra asked.

"I started noticing a few years ago. She'd forget little things. I brushed it off for a long time." He hadn't wanted to accept it. He still didn't.

"Mom and I used to watch old movies with her," Myra said. Skyler's gaze found hers. "With my grandma. The movies seemed to let her mind go back to a place that was easier to remember. Especially Christmas movies. I think we watched *It's a Wonderful Life* about a hundred times the year before she passed." She clutched her tea like it was anchoring her. "It's still my favorite movie."

He stilled, not sure what to say. That was exactly why he sang the same songs over and over.

"Anyhow," Myra tapped her fingers on the ceramic mug. "I didn't mean to pry. I just thought—"

"I sing her favorite songs to her every night." The words fell out of his mouth. He almost caught them with his hand. "Even when I'm on the road. Carol will bring me up on a video call."

Myra's mouth shifted into a soft, genuine smile. "I'm sure that helps her."

"I hope so."

The grandfather clock in the living room gonged, signaling the top of the hour.

Myra straightened. "I should really be going." She stood from the stool, and Skyler realized it had to be seven o'clock. Outside, the sun was setting over the lake.

"I hope I didn't keep you from your kids."

She shook her head and carried her mug to the sink. "No. They're with their father tonight. My ex."

"Oh." For a moment, Skyler wondered how long Myra and her ex had been separated. This was the first she'd mentioned of him.

"We share custody." She set the mug in the sink. "He wanted to take them out to dinner tonight." She looked like she had more to say but closed her mouth and gathered her keys from the island. "I'm going to head back to the barn for a bit."

With the change of subject, Skyler realized there was no reason to be concerned about Myra's ex. That was her business. He should respect her privacy.

"Spend some time with Prince Charming?" he asked, wanting to lighten the mood.

She smiled at his question. "Yes. And then I have an important date with a glass of wine at home."

"Sounds like a good night."

"Thanks for the tea," she said. "Do you need a ride back to your car?"

"Nah. I'll get it tomorrow," he replied. "I'll ride with Carol when she goes into town to get groceries."

Myra looked concerned. "But won't that leave your grandma alone?"

"I've got a few nurses on staff for her." Carol had been with him the longest, and he trusted her like family, but Skyler had three other caretakers on his payroll.

"Okay." The keys jingled in her hand. "Good."

"I'll walk you to the door," Skyler offered. He led the way out of the kitchen and through the living room, which still contained boxes that needed to be unpacked. Bypassing them, he opened the front door. "And if you have time tomorrow, I'd like to go through some files with you. After closing? I have some questions about some of the records I went through today."

"Sure." Myra walked out onto the front deck. "I'll be free until the kids get out of school." She turned to leave.

"Myra?"

She stopped on the stairs, and her black braid shimmied across her back. "Yes?"

"Thank you for your help today."

Her eyebrows drew together, almost puzzled. "Of course."

Chapter Nine

"So, when do I get to meet him?" Becca whispered excitedly before topping off two mugs with steamed milk. Her short blonde hair was pulled half up into a tiny bun. She wore a flowy cardigan over black leggings printed with yellow smiley faces, which perfectly matched her personality. Becca was the eternal optimist. Myra admired her positive attitude. It evened out Myra's cynicism.

"I guess whenever he shows his face to you," Myra replied.

She hadn't meant to tell Becca who the "silent partner" was, but Judy had spilled the beans. Keeping her mother quiet was proving harder than she'd anticipated. Judy was dying to call everyone in her Rolodex and tell them that Skyler Ridge—yes, *that* Skyler Ridge—had invested some of his Nashville-earned money in her daughter's coffee shop.

"Remember, we're supposed to keep it quiet. He's trying to keep a low profile." At least until Myra threw him into a situation where the paparazzi could take pictures of him. Her chest tightened at the thought.

After her time with Skyler last night, Myra had gotten the hunch that he was more private than he let on. After she got home, Myra had sat on her couch with a glass of wine and googled Skyler Ridge. She'd discovered plenty of pictures and videos of concerts and red carpets. Many showed his ex-wife, Cassidy Kane, who was a total knockout. Apparently, Skyler had met her while shooting a music video. She'd been a backup dancer, and they'd wed after a month. They'd been married for a few years and had looked enamored with each other—early in their relationship. But the most recent stories said they'd divorced not long after she'd been cast in a movie. And now she was dating the director of said movie. Myra cringed, making her own assumptions about what had happened. She knew marriage wasn't easy. And it certainly wouldn't work if both people weren't in it for the right reasons.

But while Myra had found plenty of information about Skyler's broken marriage, his music, and every event he attended, she'd seen very few mentions of his grandma. And the only information she'd found about his life pre-fame was what had recently been leaked to the press.

Now Cedric's plan wasn't sitting well with her. It didn't seem right. Especially because Cedric was keeping it a secret from Skyler.

"I don't know how you even concentrate around that man. He's gorgeous." Becca interrupted Myra's thoughts. She cocked her head at Myra while sprinkling dashes of cinnamon on the lattes. "And totally your type."

Myra's right eyebrow rose halfway up her forehead. She knew exactly what Becca was referring to. Her ex-husband had also been gorgeous, wild, and completely bad for her.

"Not anymore." Myra patted Becca on the shoulder. "In fact, you can have dibs on all the bad boys. No more for me. Thank you very much." *If* she ever dated again, it would be someone completely the opposite of her ex-husband. She didn't need that rollercoaster again. If she let a man into her life, she wanted something closer to a Ferris wheel. Or maybe a Tilt-a-Whirl. She did need a *little* excitement. "And if you're looking for advice from someone who's been there, go after a nice guy." Myra was protective of Becca, like a big sister.

"Oh, I didn't say I wanted dibs on him. Or any guy, for that matter." She wrinkled her nose. "But that's why I need you to tell me what he's like. I just want to live vicariously through you. A girl can dream, right?"

Myra took the finished lattes from Becca. She wasn't going to egg Becca on. Was Skyler handsome? *Yes.* But Myra was not about to get swept away by a handsome face and chiseled arms. She had about a million reasons not to do so. "He's just a man who wanted to make an investment."

Becca looked disappointed. "Oh, come on. Throw a girl a bone. It's not often we get fresh pickings here in Maple Bay. And especially pickings that look like *him*."

Myra laughed. "Honestly, we haven't even spent that much time together."

"Well, you need to."

Myra gave Becca a playful shake of her head. Then she set the lattes in front of Patty and Kandi at their table at the front of the shop, the designated gossip-sharing pit stop for Eleanor and other spry ladies of a certain age. Eleanor already had her peppermint mocha.

"There you go, ladies." Myra smiled. "Can I get you anything else?"

"Just the name of that handsome man you were driving around with yesterday." Eleanor winked and sipped her mocha like she'd accidentally thrown a leg trap at Myra's feet.

"Driving around with?" Myra opted to act confused.

"Isn't he the same guy who was in here the other morning with Chad?" Kandi asked. She prodded a little more demurely than Eleanor.

Patty leaned over the table. "And that bought the Churches' cabin on the lake?"

What was this? Amateur sleuthing hour? If Skyler had moved to a small town to flee from prying eyes, he didn't know what he was in for. The paparazzi had nothing on the Maple Bay gossip train. It was only a matter of time before the whole town knew that Skyler Ridge was here.

But Myra wasn't going to be the one to tell them. "You know, if I ever need a detective, I'll just hire you ladies instead."

Eleanor looked excited by this, but then waggled her finger. "You didn't answer our questions."

Myra sashayed away from the table. "What fun would that be?" She went back behind the counter, figuring the ladies would track down Skyler on their own. She knew they were harmless. Mostly.

But the ladies had made one thing clear: no one in Maple Bay was going to turn a blind eye to a newcomer. As the morning clicked on, Myra wondered what that would mean for Skyler. If he had come here looking for anonymity, would he disappear as soon as the town turned a spotlight on him? And honestly, was he trying that hard to hide? She knew what Cedric's plan was—to get Skyler back in the good graces of his fans and his label. But what was Skyler's plan?

"Momma, why do we have to wash the dishes before we put them in the dishwasher?" Finch asked as he ran a plate under the faucet and then handed it to his sister.

"Yeah, why? It seems totally counterproductive." Paisley put the wet plate into the rack. "I mean, it's called a dish-*washer*, right?"

"You guys are lucky you don't have to wash them all by hand like I did when I was a kid." Myra opened the fridge. She looked for a spot to stash the container of leftovers, but the fridge was at capacity—much like their apartment. Three people in a two-bedroom with one bathroom sometimes felt cozy. Other times, it felt like a stew pot ready to blow. Especially with a teenager in the house. "Besides, I don't want to empty the dishwasher tomorrow and have caked-on gunk all over the *clean* dishes. Do you think there are little elves in there that scrub the dishes for you?"

Finch giggled and ran a glass under the water. "That'd be funny."

Paisley rolled her eyes, and Myra decided to pretend she was rolling them at her brother.

"Get it done, and we can have ice cream." She shut the fridge and grabbed the second container of leftovers that sat on the counter. "I'm going to run this over to Grandma's. I expect this kitchen clean when I get back."

"I wish we had elves," Finch said, and giggled. Paisley sighed, and Myra headed for the door. As she trudged down the stairs, she wondered why God gave teenagers an explosion of hormones they didn't know how to handle. Having a teenage daughter was like having a cat. Paisley could be sweet and cuddly. But most of the time, she was only willing to come out of her bedroom to eat. She also hissed at Myra for no good reason.

"I hope Finchy never hits puberty," she mumbled, but jolted out of her own head when she spotted light at the bottom of the stairs. *I thought I turned everything off in the shop.* Myra made her way down the rest of the stairs and discovered the light was coming from the office. The door was open. Skyler sat at the desk, looking intently at papers before his gaze flitted up to find hers.

"Hey," she said, suddenly aware she was wearing her favorite yoga pants and thermal shirt. Both of which were threadbare and sported a couple of holes. They were beyond comfy, but not what she would normally wear in front of company. "I didn't know you were down here." She shifted her weight onto one foot, awkwardly. At least she was wearing a bra.

"I wanted to finish looking through some files." He stared at her through dark-rimmed glasses, and Myra thought he had a little Clark Kent thing going on. His hair was damp and pushed back from his face; he must've taken a shower just before coming over. Her stomach fluttered, and her mind immediately squashed its silly reaction.

"I'm taking some leftovers to my mom's. She's playing bridge tonight but should be home soon." Not that he needed to know any of that. "Anyhow, I'll let you be." Obviously, he had shown up late in the evening when no one would be in the shop. He wanted privacy.

She turned to leave but stopped when Skyler spoke.

"Hey, Myra. Can you tell me anything about this picture?"

Myra stepped into the office. "Picture?" A black-and-white photo rested on the desk. It lay on top of the files he'd been perusing yesterday. "Oh, wow. I forgot I even had that." She stepped around the back of the desk and stood next to Skyler, getting a better look at the photo that had been hidden away in her files.

"It was in a folder with the mortgage paperwork," Skyler said.

Myra prickled at the reminder of the bills she hadn't been able to pay, but quickly pushed away her ache. "I must've put it in there after the sale. The last owner gave the photo to me. Alan Walt. He's the one that converted the barn into a living space. He lived in the apartment upstairs and used the main level as a garage, but sold the place to me when he moved out of state to be closer to his grandkids." Myra touched the edge of the photo. It showed the barn in its original state as a dairy barn. A man and a woman stood in front of the barn with a Holstein cow. "I believe this is a picture of the original owners. The couple that built the barn."

"Do you know their names?" Skyler asked.

Myra's eyebrows raised. Why was he so interested in the history of the building?

"I don't, but I bet there are records at the library. I could also ask my mom or grandpa if they knew the original owners."

"That'd be great," Skyler replied flatly. "I'll check with the library as well."

Myra's curiosity got the best of her, and she started to ask him why he was so concerned with the original owners, but a whinnying noise cut off her thought.

Skyler sat back. His chair rolled a few inches with the quick movement. "Was that a *horse?*"

She glanced at him just as a second, higher-pitched whinny came—also from the other side of the wall. "Actually, it's two horses."

Skyler blinked up at her like he couldn't tell if she was pulling his leg. "Really? Where?"

"In the paddock behind the shop. Tomorrow is Pet-A-Pony-Saturday." Her quick explanation seemed to confuse him further. "On Fridays, I usually ride Charm over from my aunt and uncle's place. As long as the weather is nice. Then, on Saturday, customers can visit and pet him. Charm is a big attraction. Parents and grandparents love to bring their kids to see him. And they grab a cup of coffee when they stop over. Plus, this time I also brought Princess Sparkle Sugar Cookie. Finchy rode her into town, alongside me and Charm."

"*Princess Sparkle Sugar Cookie?*" Skyler's repetition made the pony's name sound crazy.

Myra smirked. "It's my niece Charlie's pony. Charlie named her, but honestly, the name fits."

The high-pitched whinny came again.

"Are they okay back there?" Skyler's voice rose. Myra wasn't sure if he was disturbed or concerned.

"They're fine. It's just their way of making sure I know they'd like more hay." She stepped out from behind the desk and stood in the doorway. "I was going to throw them a few flakes on my way over to my mom's."

"I feel like I need to see this."

"The horses?"

"It's not every day I get to see a couple of horses hanging out at a coffee shop."

Myra shrugged. "Depends on where you live. It's the norm around here."

Skyler huffed a laugh. He followed her down the hall toward the back of the shop. As soon as Myra opened the door, both Charm and Princess whinnied loudly, like they couldn't believe she had taken so long to come at their beck and call.

"Hey, you cute little piggies," Myra said affectionately.

From behind her, Skyler said, "They look hungry."

"Don't let them fool you. They've already had plenty of hay. I'm just going to give them a snack."

Charm arched his elegant neck over the top of the paddock fence, looking like the regal prince that he was. His coat shone silver in the last of the setting sun. Princess was about half the size of Charm and genuinely resembled a pony-sized sugar cookie. Her golden coat was topped off with a sugar-white mane and tail. She impatiently stuck her head between the fence boards and gave Myra a nicker.

Myra set the container of leftovers on one of the patio tables and walked over to the paddock. She rubbed Charm on his forehead and scratched Princess near the base of her ears—their favorite places. Skyler stayed a few steps behind her.

"I promise they're not mean." Myra wasn't sure how anyone could be leery of horses. Sure, they were big. Precautions were needed, but horses offered so much . . . love, connection, freedom. She didn't want anyone to fear such a magical animal. It was one of the reasons she shared her horse with the community—so everyone got a chance to enjoy them.

"They don't *look* mean," Skyler replied before stepping up next to Myra. "It's just that I've been stepped on, bit, and thrown from the saddle. All in the name of country music. And I don't want those things to happen again."

Myra winced. "Well, these two are pretty well behaved. Otherwise, I wouldn't bring them here for kiddos to love on."

Skyler tentatively reached out and petted Princess on her forehead. Then he followed Myra's cue and scratched close to the pony's ear. Princess tipped her head and leaned into his scratches. "You like that, huh?"

"She does. She'll stand there forever if you just scratch her." The little pony's eyes blinked and nearly closed as Skyler rubbed her. Charm stretched his neck over the fence and nudged Skyler's shoulder with his muzzle. He wanted attention as well.

"Hey." Skyler laughed. He rubbed Charm between his brown eyes.

"See? They're not so bad."

"Yeah. You're right. Nobody's tried to bite me *yet*."

Myra smirked and patted Charm on the neck. "Horses are honest creatures. They don't know any other way to be. As long as you're honest and true, they'll respect you." Myra stilled as her own words hit her ears. Skyler had been called a liar by the tabloids about a million times in the past week. The two things he hadn't been called were honest or true.

Skyler cleared his throat. "You think the horses know I'm not a cowboy?"

Myra dropped her hand from Charm's neck. Skyler's question felt more like an admission than an inquiry. She thought about telling him that a horse could spot a fake from miles away, that they saw past facades and words. Instead, she asked a question. "Why pretend to be someone you're not?" In Myra's eyes, that was wasted energy.

"Because I wanted to sing." He took off his glasses and hooked them on the front of his shirt. "When my label signed me, they did it on one condition. I was to fill a slot in their catalog and follow their rules."

"What kind of rules?"

"I was asked to play a part, sing the type of music they wanted me to. Essentially, the label molded me into what they thought country music needed. They created a brand. A persona. And they weren't wrong. Skyler Ridge was what the market wanted."

A black swallow darted out from under the barn rafter and disappeared into the evening sky. "But it wasn't what you wanted?" she asked.

"It was." He hooked a thumb in his jeans pocket. "I wanted my songs on the radio. To play music in front of thousands of people. I thought I needed the notoriety that comes with a big-name label. And I got all of that. It's just that I lost myself somewhere along the way." He draped an arm over the top rail of the fence. The horses stood quietly, sensing the seriousness of the conversation. Skyler broke the quiet with a chuckle under his breath. "It sounds so stupid when I say it out loud. I don't mean to complain about having a job most people would kill for. I love music. It's just that I'm ready to do it my way."

"It's not stupid," Myra said. Skyler's posture had changed as though he needed to lean against something. He was holding himself up through force of will. "You feel like the real you isn't good enough." She knew that feeling. During her marriage, she'd felt like she wasn't the wife or mother she was supposed to be. And she'd stayed in that place for far too long.

Skyler turned his head toward her. He gave an awkward nod and pushed himself off from the fence. "Where do you keep the hay for these horses?" He glanced around, obviously wanting to change the subject.

"Oh, yeah. The hay." Myra ran a hand over Charm's muzzle. "I keep a few bales in the shed." She pointed toward the shed at the back of the shop, and Charm's head shot up. His ears pricked forward, and Myra turned to see what her horse was gawking at. As she did, Myra saw someone across the street—a woman who was partially hidden behind the edge of a tall fence. Myra also spotted the end of a long camera lens.

Was that . . . paparazzi? Was that the photographer Cedric sent?

"What are you looking at, Charm?" Skyler turned toward the half-hidden photographer. Myra gasped and grabbed his arm, spinning Skyler back toward the horses. In her haste, she kicked the toe of his boot and stumbled. Skyler caught her. He hooked an arm around her middle and slid his hand over her lower back. If they'd been dancing, Myra would've expected him to dip her with his next move.

"You okay?" His amber gaze flicked over her face. His arm was strong and warm, slung around her ribcage and back.

"Yeah," she exhaled. When her lungs refilled, she cursed her sense of smell. Being this close to Skyler, she wondered if his label had branded his scent as well. Because he smelled like the country. Clean and crisp like an autumn morning or an impromptu gallop through a field.

Skyler set his other hand on her arm, breaking her from the momentary hypnosis.

"Clumsy me." Myra laughed nervously. She peeked past his shoulder. The photographer was gone. Or at least out of sight. She fumbled to give Skyler a reason for her swift reaction. "There was a huge mosquito on your neck. I don't know if you guys have mosquitos in Nashville, but the mosquitos in Minnesota are serious business. I was trying to save you from getting bit." She stood up and reached for his neck, trying to show him where the fictitious mosquito had landed. However, Myra had misjudged what would happen to her when she ran her fingers over his neck. Especially because his hand was still pressed to the small of her back.

A spark flickered in her chest—a jolt Myra wasn't used to. She jerked her hand away like she'd grazed an electric fence.

"All right." Skyler said the words slowly, as though he wasn't quite sure what had just happened. "Thank you?"

"You're welcome." Myra forced a cheerful tone. She spun out of Skyler's hold and away from the uninvited sensations that had infiltrated her body. She walked straight to the shed, yanked open the door, and grabbed two flakes of hay from an open bale. Turning, she launched the hay over the fence and into the paddock, where Charm and Princess were staring at her with knowing eyes. She was certain they saw straight through her lies.

Chapter Ten

The next morning, Skyler stared out his kitchen window as he pushed eggs around in a frying pan. He should've been thinking about the coffee shop, what he was going to do with the disaster that had become his music career, or what excuse he'd give Cedric the next time he called. Instead, his mind kept winding its way back to Myra Wilder. Yesterday, he'd surprised himself when he'd talked to her about a topic that he always kept close to his chest. In fact, he'd only talked about his grandma's dementia to his band, Cassidy, and Cedric. However, there was something about Myra that put him at ease, pushed him to open up. At least, it had in that moment.

Furthermore, he couldn't ignore how he'd felt the other night when she'd stumbled into his arms. He'd only meant to catch her, but Myra's proximity had jolted him awake as if he'd been startled from a nap. The spark was unexpected and unwanted, but now that his eyes had been opened, he wasn't sure he could fall back asleep.

Skyler added a few dashes of salt and pepper to the scrambled eggs, excusing away his rash thoughts. Myra hadn't meant to fall into his arms. It had obviously been far too long since he'd held a woman—six months since his divorce and much longer since he'd shared any type of intimacy. He'd lost faith in Cassidy well before the divorce papers were signed. He'd thought they were in love. Otherwise, he never would have married her. But it had turned out that his instincts were far from right. The only things she'd ever truly loved were Skyler's fame and pocketbook.

Turning off the burner, Skyler shook his head at himself. He shouldn't be examining how Myra felt in his arms. He did *not* intend to get wrapped up in anything—not an embrace or a fling. And certainly not a relationship. Besides, Myra was his employee. He shouldn't be thinking of her in any way other than as the shop's manager. That was inappropriate. And distracting.

"Oh, Sky. You didn't have to make me breakfast," Dorthea said as she walked into the kitchen. "I should be cooking for you."

Sky glanced over his shoulder and smiled at his grandma. She was dressed in khaki slacks and a pink cardigan. Her white hair was coifed and curled under at her chin, and her lips shone with rose-colored lipstick. She'd never been the type of woman to wear sweatpants or pajamas outside the bedroom. When she woke up, she got dressed and ready for the day.

"You know I love to spoil you." Skyler took two plates out of the cupboard and scooped scrambled eggs on each. He'd given

Dorthea's caregivers the day off, and it was nice to have a quiet house—a space that only he and his grandma shared. Her caregivers did an amazing job, and Skyler was lucky to have them. Each had moved from Nashville to Maple Bay to continue caring for his grandma. But he relished having his own space for a day. Cassidy had filled their house with maids, cooks, assistants, and security. Skyler had constantly felt overwhelmed in his own home. He hadn't even had space to think. Now he was getting the privacy he'd been craving for some time. "Why don't you take a seat, and I'll bring breakfast to you?"

"My sweet boy." Dorthea walked over and got comfortable at the big oak table.

He added a few pieces of crispy bacon to each plate. "Tea or orange juice?" he asked, setting a plate in front of his grandma. She didn't respond. Dorthea was staring down at the black-and-white photograph he'd found in Myra's files. Skyler had brought the picture home and placed it on the table.

Skyler set the other plate down without taking his eyes off his grandma's face. Her forehead creased, like she was trying hard to place the couple in the picture.

"Who's this?" she asked and looked to Skyler. His heart fell. Dorthea seemed to remember the past better than the present. He'd hoped the photo would spark a memory she'd share with him.

"An old photo I found." He walked to the stove, deciding she'd like tea. As he prepared it, the kitchen stayed quiet. He wouldn't press his grandma about the photo. His intention wasn't to frustrate her with memories she couldn't place. Maybe she didn't know the couple in the photo, but he'd thought she'd recognize the barn. She'd recognized it when they'd driven by the building a few months ago.

This past winter, Skyler had been part of a "hometown concert series" his label had organized. It was a handful of concerts in small towns across the Midwest. He and his band had hit the road, playing in bars, auditoriums, and even an outdoor rodeo arena, where it had snowed. Skyler had brought Dorthea along on the tour—along with her nurse, Carol. He hadn't felt right about leaving his grandma in Nashville, and she loved to watch his concerts, so he had rented an extra tour bus with all the bells and whistles, just for Dorthea and Carol. They'd had their own space, filled with all the necessities and luxuries needed to keep them comfortable.

The concert in the rodeo arena—the one where big snowflakes had fallen as he had sung to the crowd—had been in Sugar Springs, just an hour north of Maple Bay. Since Dorthea had grown up on a farm in southern Minnesota, Skyler had thought it'd be fun to take her for a country drive that next day, just the two of them. Her face had lit up as they'd careened past farms and livestock. She'd pointed to horses and tractors and told him stories from her childhood. They'd ended up in Maple Bay, where they'd had lunch at a fifties-style drive-in diner and then cruised along the lake, following the road that led them to the quaint downtown. When they'd come upon Perkup Coffee, Dorthea had reached over and squeezed Skyler's arm, asking him to stop. He'd parked on the road, right in front of the shop.

She'd stared, intently focused on the coffee shop. "I've been here. A long, long time ago. There was a wedding. My friend got married here." Then she put her hands to her chest, gave a deep sigh, and smiled from ear to ear. "Oh, we danced the whole night away."

Dorthea had mentioned a three-tiered wedding cake and told Skyler of the band that had played all her favorite songs. She'd dreamily described the ceremony along the lakeshore. Her happiness had made Skyler smile, especially because he'd also recognized the barn that was now a coffee shop. He'd realized it was the same barn in the black-and-white photo of his grandma when she was young—a photo that had always held a prominent place in her house. It had decorated the wall in the dining room for as long as Skyler could remember.

But now, as Dorthea stared at the old picture lying before her on the kitchen table, Skyler didn't see that same recognition on her face.

He set a mug of tea next to her plate. "It's just a barn in the area. A friend gave the photo to me. I thought it would remind you of your childhood farm." He sat down, not wanting to upset her. Maybe the photo would spark a memory another day?

"So sweet of you. I love it." She patted his hand. Skyler gave her a smile, but devastation gripped the pit of his stomach. How long did he have before all her memories slipped away? Had this all been for nothing? Was there *anything* he could do?

The next day, Skyler stopped by Perkup mid-morning, knowing that Myra didn't open the shop on Sundays. He took advantage of the peace and quiet to further dig through her records and see if he could better understand how she'd fallen so far in the hole financially. But he couldn't connect the dots. Had he bought a cash cow? No, but it looked to be a sustainable business. With a few tweaks, the café could be profitable.

After making a few notes, Skyler decided he needed caffeine. Leaving the office, he made his way into the shop, rummaged through a few cabinets, and found an open bag of coffee beans. He prepped half a pot and leaned back on the counter as it brewed, looking around the dining area. It wasn't anything fancy, but it was cozy. *Homey.* There were maybe ten tables of various sizes and shapes. The chairs that surrounded them were wooden and mismatched. Red-and-white checkered valances hung at the top of each window. Western décor peppered the walls: a coat rack made of metal horseshoes, framed vintage rodeo posters, antiqued bits and bridles. The Western theme fit the remodeled barn. It also fit Myra.

After the coffee finished brewing, Skyler poured himself a mug. As he took his first sip, the back door opened. Footsteps fell against the wooden floor, and Finch ran out of the hall.

"Hey, Skyler!" he shout-greeted. "Whatcha doing?" Finch sported a wide grin, pressed jeans, and a collared shirt. His dark hair was slicked to the side.

"Hey, there." Skyler couldn't help but grin at the kid's enthusiasm. It was contagious. "I was just doing a little work, but now I'm taking a coffee break. What're you up to?"

"Just got done with church, so Mom said I can put my scrubby clothes back on."

Skyler chuckled. "Is that so?"

"Yeah, church clothes aren't very comfy," Finch replied. "Plus, I'm not supposed to get 'em dirty."

Myra appeared from the hall. "Which is why you'd better change if you want to go fishing."

Skyler had taken another slug of coffee and nearly spit it out when he got an eyeful of Myra. Her dark hair fell over her shoulder and across her chest in a soft wave. She wore a turquoise wrap dress that perfectly matched her eyes. Like Finch, she also wore cowboy boots, but hers were sandy brown and inlaid with intricate leather stamping. Skyler suddenly realized how much her T-shirts had hidden her curves.

Skyler swallowed his coffee in a hard lump. He blurted the first thing he thought to say. "Church, huh?"

"Cowboy church," Myra replied. "The first one of the season. When the weather is decent, there's a second Sunday service held at the fairgrounds."

Finch held his hand up to his mouth like he was telling Skyler a secret. "I like it a lot better than being *in* the church."

Skyler grinned. "Sounds interesting. Do you ride?"

"I sure do, but I don't ride during cowboy church. Not yet, anyhow. Sometimes Momma does though." Finch looked up at

Myra with admiration. "Sometimes she rides Charm and carries the flag."

"Not today, obviously." Myra smiled at her son and swished her skirt with her hand. Visions of Myra in the saddle assaulted Skyler's mind. "But I'm riding next Sunday."

"You should come!" Finch offered.

Myra's gaze hit Skyler's. "You should. Everyone is welcome. You could bring Dorthea."

Skyler hadn't been to church in years. In fact, the last time had been back in high school, with his grandparents. "I think she'd love that. I might take you up on that offer next weekend."

"You could even sing if you want," Finch added excitedly. "There's already a guy that plays guitar. His name is Tim. But you could play with him."

Both Myra and Skyler laughed.

"Maybe someday," Skyler said, and that was enough to satisfy Finch.

"Okay, I'd better go change so I can go fishing." Finch tore off toward the stairs.

Myra called after him. "Remind your sister that Grandma wants her help in the kitchen."

A myriad of stair-pounding noises echoed in the hall. Then Paisley poked her head out of the hallway. "I'm headed over there now." She gave a timid smile and a wave to Skyler. He waved back. Paisley seemed much shyer than her brother.

"Thanks, baby." Myra strode into the shop as Paisley disappeared. "Did you make coffee?" She took a deep breath, like she desperately needed a cup.

"I did."

"You read my mind." Myra took a mug off a hook under the cabinets. It was bright purple, sparkly, and read *Momma Needs More Coffee*. She filled it to the tip-top and took a long slurp. Steam curled over her lips, and Skyler caught himself staring. When she lowered the mug from her mouth, she asked, "What? Do I have something on my face?" She touched her cheek.

Skyler gave a quick shake of his head. "Nah. Just admiring your coffee cup." Especially as it was pressed to her lips.

"Oh, thanks." She raised the mug. "The kids gave it to me for Christmas. It's my favorite." She took another drink. Then a glimmer of worry passed over her face. "Did you need something? I told you that I close Perkup on Sundays, right?"

"Yeah," he reassured her. "I was just doing some paperwork."

"Okay, good. Finding what you're looking for?"

"Yes. Well, kind of." He shifted against the counter. "I was reviewing sales reports and trying to figure out the reason behind the decrease in the past year. Was it related to anything in particular?"

Myra held the steaming mug just below her chin. She gave a little sigh. "Another coffee shop opened on the north side of the lake this past fall. Naomi's Kwik Coffee."

"Is that the drive-through place?"

Myra nodded. "It attracts a lot of the younger crowd. They make all these concoctions. Smoothies with energy drinks. Frappuccinos with more sugar than a bucket of frosting. But their actual coffee tastes like dirt." The disgust on her face told Skyler she'd rather drink sour milk.

Skyler raised a brow. "But clearly they're doing something right if they're taking business from Perkup. Right? Is there something we could add to the menu to compete with them?"

Myra pursed her lips. "I mean . . . I have some ideas. I've wanted to add a weekly coffee special to the menu for a while now but just haven't had time to play around with recipes. Plus, the regulars are pretty set on what I already offer."

"But how do you know they wouldn't like something new unless you try? Why don't we play around with some recipes right now?"

"Now? We?"

"Sure. I have no idea how to run this"—Skyler waved a hand at the very complicated-looking espresso machine—"but I can be your sous-chef. And I'm a good taste-tester."

The reluctance on Myra's face shifted to curiosity. She took a long sip from her sparkly purple mug before setting it on the counter. "I've got an hour. I'll get us some aprons."

Chapter Eleven

"I keep the most popular syrups and ingredients on hand, based on sales," Myra explained as she pulled bottles out from the cabinet under the espresso machine. She set them on the counter, one by one. "But I have a personal stash for when I need an extra special pick-me-up." After she'd retrieved a half dozen bottles, Myra reached to the very back of the cabinet and grabbed a container. She clutched it to her chest.

"What do you have there?" Skyler asked.

"My secret chocolate stash." Myra stood up.

Skyler grinned at her, looking amused. "You have a secret chocolate stash?"

"Doesn't every mother?" She set the container next to the espresso machine and gave him a look like he should know that. Skyler laughed. "What? There are some things the kids don't need to know about. And there are some days that require chocolate."

"I completely agree." He grabbed three latte mugs out of the cabinet and put them on the counter near the syrups. "Is that enough?"

"Yeah, that should be good." Myra filled one of the portafilters with freshly ground coffee. Then she pressed the grounds into the basket with a tamper.

When she clicked the portafilter into the espresso machine, Skyler asked, "What can I do?"

"There's a metal jigger over there." She directed him with a nod of her head. "You can add the syrups. In the first mug, can you put an ounce of blueberry syrup, half an ounce of lemon, and half an ounce of vanilla?"

Skyler arched an eyebrow in interest. He started measuring and pouring as Myra steamed the milk.

"And the next one?" He placed the first mug in front of the espresso machine.

Myra continued steaming the milk, watching it froth. "An ounce of lavender and a half ounce of toasted coconut."

"My mouth is starting to water," he said, following her instructions.

Myra grinned. A coconut-lavender latte was her absolute favorite. In a few sips, the lavender always managed to ease her mind and soothe her nerves. The coconut flavor and creamy milk also satisfied her sweet tooth. "And in the last one, put . . ." She glanced over at the bottles, taking stock of what she had. "Mmmm . . . blackberry and maple? An ounce of each." The combination struck her in an instant. "Oh, goodness. I can't believe I haven't made that before. That sounds scrumptious." Her eyes widened at the thought.

Skyler looked apprehensive. "That last one seems... *interesting*."

"Let's give it a try."

He finished adding the syrups and placed the other mugs in front of the espresso machine. Myra poured the frothed milk into each mug, watching it fold on itself.

"Can you grab the whipped cream? It's in the fridge." Myra set all three mugs in the espresso machine and pulled double shots for each. As the shop filled with the rich aroma of coffee, she opened her secret-chocolate-stash container and nosed through, looking for the dark chocolate. When Skyler appeared with a can of whipped cream, she pulled the first mug out from the espresso machine. "Go ahead and add some whip."

To Myra's surprise, the can immediately hissed, and a mountain of whipped cream piled on top of the blueberry-lemon-vanilla latte. Myra glanced over to find Skyler holding the can like it was a fire hose that he needed two hands to control.

"I might've gone a little overboard." A dollop of cream rolled down the side of the mug. Skyler grinned.

Myra laughed. "I do love whipped cream, but maybe a little less on the others. So we can taste the latte part."

"If you say so." Skyler winked and added a smaller swirl of cream to the other mugs.

"I usually only make these special lattes for my girlfriends. As a treat." Myra opened a bar of dark chocolate and snatched a knife out of a drawer. She shaved off some chocolate and sprinkled it on top of each of the drinks, realizing she hadn't made her special treats in quite some time. It seemed she was always running from one thing to the next, trying to stay on top of . . . life. If it wasn't the shop that needed her attention, it was her kids, mom, or the endless number of chores to keep up on. "Plus, I don't like to keep too many syrups and extras around the shop that don't get used on a regular basis." She hadn't had the extra cash to do so either.

"Well, these look pretty good." Skyler set the whipped cream can down. "Which should we try first?"

"You pick."

He squinted at the mugs. "Let's try the maple-blackberry first." He raised the mug to his lips, peered at it, and took a sip. As he swallowed, a surprised expression hit his face. "Wow."

"Is that a good *wow* or a bad *wow*?"

He offered the mug to her. "Try it."

Myra took the latte and sipped from the opposite side than Skyler had. The tartness of the blackberry hit her tongue and was quickly complemented by the cream and sweet maple. She closed her eyes, enjoying the burst of flavor and indulgence. Appreciation slipped out of her throat in the form of a little purr.

"Oh, that's a winner." She opened her eyes. Skyler was staring at her—zoned in on her, almost like *she* was the latte. Her stomach fluttered, and she held his gaze, even though her mind told her to look away. "Don't you think?"

He broke his stare with a blink. "Yeah. Amazing, actually."

"The flavors really pair well with each other." Myra had both hands wrapped around the mug, holding it just below her chin.

She took another sip. This time, she kept her eyes open, watching Skyler. She swallowed. "Try the lavender-coconut latte." She offered him the other mug, and his fingers grazed hers in the exchange. Her stomach did that fluttery thing again. She wished it would stop.

Skyler sipped. "I don't think I've ever *tasted* anything with lavender in it, but that is delicious. Perfect with the coconut and dark chocolate pieces." He licked a smudge of whipped cream from his upper lip.

"It's my favorite, actually."

"I still think the blackberry-maple beats it."

"Really? You were so skeptical of that combo."

"There's something really intriguing about the initial sour followed by the unexpected sweetness." Skyler gave a shoulder shrug. His eyes were on her again. "I guess I've got a thing for that combination. It caught my attention."

The way he was looking at her, she wondered if he was still talking about the latte. Was he . . . was he talking about her? Had he called her sour and then unexpectedly sweet? Said that she'd caught his attention? Myra broke their gaze. She was overthinking his comment. *He's just talking about a latte.* Skyler Ridge could have any woman he wanted. He wasn't interested in her—romantically, anyhow. Skyler was interested in how she ran Perkup and what kind of profits she could make for him.

Frazzled by her out-of-the-blue thoughts, Myra grabbed the blueberry-lemon-vanilla latte and raised it to her lips, momentarily forgetting how much whipped cream Skyler had added to that mug. When the cool topping hit her skin, she jerked back and froze. She'd just dipped her nose in cream.

A smile crept across his face. "I had a heavy hand with that one."

"You think?" Myra laughed. She reached for the towel hanging next to the espresso machine and dabbed it on her face, blindly wiping at the mess.

Skyler stared at her. "You missed a few spots."

She wiped at her nose again, hoping she didn't have cream up a nostril. "Did I get it now?"

"Most of it. But there's a schmear on your cheek." He stepped toward her and ran a thumb across her skin. As he did, his palm engulfed her jaw. His fingertips brushed her ear. Then his copper gaze ran across her cheek just as his thumb had.

Myra's boots seemed cemented to the wooden floorboards. Her heart gave a thud. She squeezed the mug in one hand and the towel in the other, afraid she was going to drop them both.

"There," Skyler said. "Got it." He hadn't removed his hand from the side of her face. Her eyes fell to his lips, and in a fleeting thought, she wondered what it would feel like if he kissed her.

Footsteps pounded down the stairs.

"I can't find my fishing pole!" Finch yelled from the stairwell.

Skyler dropped his hand, and Myra realized she was holding her arms out like she might take flight. She sucked them back in, close to her sides, just as Finch ran into the shop. He'd changed into shorts and carried a tackle box, which jingled with every stride.

Myra turned toward Finch and set the mug on the counter. Heat clung to her cheek where Skyler had touched her. A distracting haze had settled on her brain. She mentally shook it away. "Did you leave it at Grandma's?"

Finch squinted like he was trying to remember. "Maybe?"

"Why don't you go check her garage?" She silently wondered when her kids would be old enough to remember where they put things. She could only keep track of so much.

It looked like a lightbulb went off in Finch's head. "Be right back!" He ran out of the shop, leaving an awkward silence in his place. Myra wanted to fill it with just about any topic to distract herself from the heart thumps she'd just felt.

"So, you really like the maple-blackberry latte?" she asked without making eye contact.

"Yeah," Skyler replied flatly. The back door slammed shut. "I think we should add it to the menu. Let's try it as this week's special."

"Great," she replied, as though nothing had just happened between the two of them. Like the thought of kissing him hadn't crossed her mind. "I'll get the syrups ordered." She headed off toward the office to use the computer—and give herself a little space.

That afternoon, Myra dropped the kids off at Joyce and Gene's house. Her aunt and uncle always hosted Sunday supper for the whole family. Judy was already there, helping to prep a feast. Usually, Myra helped cook as well, but today, her help was needed at her cousin Kat's house. While Finch and Paisley played kickball with their cousins, Myra would join her adult cousins for a painting project. Then, everyone would gather back at Joyce and Gene's for supper.

As Myra drove the mile down the road to Kat's house, her phone dinged. When she arrived, she picked up her phone and read the text.

Cedric: *We've got some good photos so far but need more. Can you get Skyler at the barn again? Maybe on a horse?*

On a horse? Was he crazy? She'd gotten Skyler to pet a horse and thought that was a feat. Plus, now that she was getting to know Skyler, she wondered if he even cared to redeem his cowboy persona. From what he'd told her, he didn't seem happy with the direction of his music career, and hadn't been even before the media had blasted his secret out to the world.

Her stomach turned in reaction to her conflicting feelings. She'd jumped on board with Cedric's plan quickly, thinking it was the answer to her prayers. But did Cedric really have Skyler's best interests in mind?

Myra stared at Cedric's text, thinking of the best way to answer.

Myra: *Are you sure this is what Skyler wants?*

Cedric: *To ride a horse? Probably not.*

Myra: *No, to keep pretending he's someone that he's not.*

Three little dots appeared on her phone. Then they disappeared, like Cedric had reconsidered what he was going to say. A minute later, he finally replied.

Cedric: *Skyler wants to sing. I know that for sure. He needs the option to re-sign with his label. Mending his reputation is the only way to make that happen. It's the only way to put Skyler in the driver's seat so I can renegotiate the contract that's best for him.*

Myra sighed, feeling sleazy for going behind Skyler's back. From what she'd seen in the past few days, she knew Skyler was more than the stories the press painted or the persona he played. But he'd also said he didn't want to give up on his music. Myra decided she needed to hear exactly what Skyler wanted—from his own mouth. Because if she wasn't helping him, she couldn't continue to participate in Cedric's plan. That wouldn't be right, even if it got her what she needed. She'd find a different way to get her shop back.

Before she decided how to reply, Cedric sent another text.

Cedric: *Let me know when you can make it happen and I'll coordinate the photographer.*

Myra replied with a single thumbs-up emoji, even though she wanted to talk to Skyler before she threw him into another photo op. Instead of explaining that to Cedric, she jumped out of her truck and headed toward Kat and Creed's house, pushing her worries to the side for now. Today, her cousin needed her.

Kat and Creed had an adorable A-frame home set on the edge of the lake. The windows were all open, and female laughter floated out. As soon as she opened the front door, her name sounded from within. One of the excited yells came from Kat. Her cousin was standing in the living room, wearing overalls and holding a wet paint roller.

"Myra!" She jogged across drop cloths and gave Myra a one-armed hug, careful to hold the paint roller far away from them both. "Now everyone is here!"

Behind Kat, in the open living room and kitchen area, the rest of the girl-cousin paint crew greeted her. Hazel sat on a kitchen chair—the only piece of furniture atop the drop cloths—looking pregnant as could be. Kat's older sister, Anne, sat cross-legged on the floor, edging the trim with a small paint brush. Frankie, their childhood friend, waved from the top rungs of a ladder propped against the wall. She was the only part of the crew that wasn't related by blood or marriage. She was family by choice.

"Hey, guys," Myra said, happy to have some girl time, even if it included running a paint roller. "Sorry I'm late. Got hung up on a project at the shop." Her heart skipped at the memory of Skyler wiping whipped cream from her cheek. She pushed it away.

"No worries. We just got started," Kat said. "What do you think of the color?"

Myra glanced around, taking in the areas that had already been started. "Love it." The paint was a soft sage green and nicely complemented the dark-stained kitchen cabinets that Kat's fiancé, Creed, had built. "Beautiful color. So relaxing."

"Hazel helped me pick it out," Kat said.

"At least I could do *something*," Hazel replied from her spot on the kitchen chair. She rested both hands on her basketball belly, looking uncomfortable. "I can't wait until this little guy arrives so I can actually do normal things again."

"I don't know if having a newborn could be referred to as going back to *normal*," Frankie said, raising her eyebrows at Hazel from the top of the ladder.

"Oh, I'm ready for all the baby stuff." Hazel smiled. "I've been waiting a long time for that. I just can't believe how nauseated I've been in this last trimester. I wasn't sick at all with Grace."

"Did you try that ginger-lemon tea I dropped off last week?" Anne asked, dipping her brush in the paint tray.

"Yep, and that does help," Hazel replied. "But only while I'm drinking it and sitting still."

Myra took a fresh roller from the pile of supplies in the middle of the room and rolled it in a paint tray. "You poor thing." She walked over and took a spot between Frankie and Kat. She put her roller on the wall and started painting. "I had morning sickness with both Finch and Paisley, but it was only in the first trimester. A few saltine crackers usually fixed it."

"I wish a few saltine crackers would do the trick." Hazel moved one hand to the top of her belly and patted it. "But it's all worth it."

"We can't wait to meet him." Kat smiled at Hazel over her shoulder.

"Before you know it, he'll be riding horses with Jesse and the girls," Myra added.

Hazel smiled, and as the conversation turned to baby names and nursery colors, Myra thought about how much she'd been through with the women in this room. They were all close in age and had experienced life's highs and lows together. *First dates. First loves.*

First births. Marriage. Divorce. Death. No matter what life had thrown their way, they'd been there for each other, and Myra was grateful for her tight-knit family. She knew not everyone was as lucky.

Which was why she felt so guilty about keeping her financial struggles a secret from her family. If she mentioned she needed help, Myra knew her family would find a way to support her, but they'd come to her rescue many times in her life. For once, she wanted to stand on her own two feet. And, this past year, when her mom had needed financial support, Myra had wanted to give it to her.

Judy had been in pain for years and was too stubborn to make a doctor's appointment. When Myra had finally convinced her mom to go to the clinic, the doctor had recommended a hip replacement. Judy had immediately dug her heels in, saying she didn't have the time or the money for surgery, but her pain only got worse. Within a few months, she struggled to walk the short distance from her house to the coffee shop. When it got to that point, Myra used every ounce of stubbornness that her mother had taught her and insisted that her mom go forward with the surgery. Myra had also insisted that she would pay for it. Did she have the extra money? No. But she hadn't let her mom know that. Judy had needed the surgery, and Myra had wanted to make it happen.

After many discussions, Judy finally gave in but insisted the money was a loan, not a gift. She would pay Myra back when she could. Myra had agreed, reluctantly, even accepting a few small payments the previous month when Judy had forced them on her.

But by that time, Myra had already been so far behind on her bills, she was being buried alive. She hadn't meant to let everything spiral out of control, but an array of hurdles had been thrown into her path all at once. Just as Judy's medical bills had started arriving, the new coffee shop had opened across town, eating into Perkup's sales. Interest rates had also spiked, ballooning the monthly payments for the adjustable-rate mortgage Myra had on the shop. Paisley had needed braces and glasses. The shop had needed a new furnace. And before Myra knew it, her credit cards were carrying a hefty load, and she was behind on her mortgage.

Yet Myra never complained to her mom or the rest of her family. She was grateful Judy's hip replacement had been successful. She didn't want her mom to feel guilty for accepting her help. Myra had also thought she could get *herself* out of the hole she'd dug . . . until the day Chad and Skyler had showed up to her shop.

"Is Paisley going to run barrels at Maple Bay Days this year?" Kat asked, knocking Myra out of her thoughts.

"Yeah, I think so." Myra stepped back from the wall and dipped her roller in fresh paint. "She wasn't quite ready last year, but she's gained a lot of confidence riding Charm since then. She rode him quite a bit over the winter. They're really starting to gel."

"I hope she does," Kat replied. "Are you going to hit any rodeos before then? Creed and I are taking the horses to the Fargo rodeo next month. We have an extra spot in the trailer if you and the kids want to go with Charm."

Myra gave Kat a smile. "Thanks, hon. I'll talk to Paisley about it." Myra didn't have a trailer—at least not to haul her horse. She had an old horse trailer she'd revamped into a mobile coffee shop, but that was no longer horse-friendly. Come to think of it, she should see if Fargo needed a coffee vendor. She could take her mobile shop over for the weekend and make extra money while Paisley rode. The rodeo entry fees wouldn't pay themselves.

Myra's phone whinnied—it was the special ringtone she had for when Paisley texted her.

"Speaking of the little devil." Myra grinned and pulled her phone from her back pocket. When she opened the text, she expected to see Paisley asking if she could visit one of her friends tonight after supper. Instead, the text contained a link to *Stars Today*—a well-known tabloid. Another text immediately followed, also from Paisley. It simply stated: *What is this about?*

Myra clicked on the link. A photo and a headline popped up. She caught herself in a gasp when she saw that the picture was of her and Skyler. It was from the other night—when Myra had ended up in Skyler's arms. Charm and Princess were posed perfectly in the background, but the horses weren't the main attraction of the snapshot.

"Oh, boy." The words trickled out of Myra's mouth. The headline read *Skyler Ridge Charms Mystery Cowgirl*. The photo made it look like they were having a romantic moment at sunset. She quickly scrolled down to see more pictures of the two of them together in her truck.

"Everything okay?" Kat asked.

Myra looked up from her phone, trying to conceal her shock. All eyes were on her. It was time to bring her cousins into the loop.

"You know that silent investor I told you guys about?" They all nodded. Myra swallowed and turned her phone around to show them what she was looking at. The squeals that ensued could've cracked the paint on the walls. She had to wait for the commotion to settle to explain that the headline was wrong. The pictures were wrong. "We aren't dating. We aren't anything. It's completely professional between the two of us. I actually just tripped and fell into his arms, and somehow this picture makes it look like something that it's not."

Though Myra couldn't ignore the way she and Skyler were looking at each other in the photo. If she didn't personally know what had happened, she would have assumed the same as her cousins.

"You *tripped and fell* into Skyler Ridge's arms?" Frankie asked, coming down from the ladder.

Kat snatched Myra's phone and zoomed in on the picture. She quirked a brow at Myra. "That doesn't look very *professional* to me." Kat smirked. Frankie, Hazel, and Anne chimed in with agreement.

"It's just a story. That's what those tabloids do. They make a fuss out of nothing," Myra replied, but also remembered how Skyler had made her feel earlier today. The butterflies he'd given her weren't professional. Was it possible the camera had caught something Myra hadn't seen? She shook her head. "I need to call Paisley and explain."

Walking out the front door, Myra dialed her daughter. After that, she'd call Cedric. This wasn't what she'd signed up for.

Chapter Twelve

Skyler was so sick of being under the microscope of fame like a pinned bug in some science experiment. It didn't matter what he did or where he went: paparazzi found him and zoomed in on his life with a lens. The media painted a story, using his life as their own personal canvas.

"I'm done," Skyler said into the phone as he drove away from his house. "You don't need to renegotiate my contract."

"What?" Cedric screeched. "What am I supposed to tell the label?"

"That I'm out. I'm done. Tell them I've gone crazy or joined a cult. That I'm done singing. Better yet, tell them that I fell in love with a cowgirl and I'm going to spend the rest of my days roping cattle. Isn't that exactly what *Stars Today* reported?" Skyler blew a breath out of his nose. How was it that the tabloids could make up a story based on assumptions and have it be believed, but he was being crucified because he wore cowboy boots but wasn't an actual cowboy? "Besides, Country Records hasn't exactly had my back lately. The second my image fell apart, they threatened to toss me out like yesterday's trash."

"I told you, I'm fixing that."

"Don't waste your time."

"Come on, Sky. You don't mean that. You're not done with music."

"Music and fame are two different things." Skyler couldn't live without music. But fame was invasive. It was sneaky. It had tempted Skyler into its grasp and then tightened down until he had nothing more to give. "I'm serious, Cedric. I don't want this. I want to be left alone. I want to live my life how I want to live it."

"But I can negotiate a better contract, get you more money. I swear."

"The money's not worth it." *Not anymore.*

"Don't make any rash decisions."

Skyler turned onto Main Street, headed toward Perkup. "Look, I've got to go. We can talk about this later."

"Later?" Cedric replied. "I don't—"

Skyler didn't let Cedric finish. He ended the call. That conversation would have gone in circles. Besides, he wanted to talk to Myra. It was one thing for the press to invade his privacy. He expected that. But to bring Myra into the mix? Unacceptable.

The story had come out yesterday, but Skyler hadn't seen it until this morning. Yesterday, after his time at the coffee shop, he'd spent the rest of the day basking in the peace of his lake house. He'd unpacked a few more boxes and played card games with his grandma and Carol. He'd even taken a nap on his deck. Apparently, he'd been so lulled by relaxation that he'd forgotten to look at his phone until this morning. His missed calls list had been full of Cedric's name, but strangely, there was nothing from Myra. Not a call or a text. He wasn't sure how she felt about being thrown into the spotlight, but he assumed she was upset. She had kids and a family. They didn't need to be surprised by the news that Myra was having a "secret tryst."

Skyler parked in one of the few open spots on Main Street, wondering if the small downtown was always this bustling at nine o'clock on a Monday morning. But as he walked toward Perkup, he sensed something was off. Every Adirondack chair on the porch was full. The front door was propped open, and a crowd milled about inside. A big crowd. There was no way this was normal. If so, Perkup's sales wouldn't have been so dismal in the reports he'd been perusing.

As Skyler got close, mouths started to drop. Whispers got louder, but Skyler didn't slow his stride. Instead of running off and hiding, he needed to face this head on. It was time to introduce himself to Maple Bay.

"Howdy," an older man in one of the Adirondack chairs greeted him.

Skyler tipped his head in greeting. "Good morning." He nodded at the rest of the Adirondack-sitters. As he stepped inside, gasps sounded. A camera clicked, and a flash went off toward the back of the shop. Skyler stopped. He spotted Myra behind the counter. Her blue eyes were wide as saucers, and her mouth hung open. A blonde woman hovered beside her, dressed in an apron and looking just as shocked. Skyler assumed that was Becca, the employee Myra had insisted Skyler keep.

Skyler waved at the crowded shop. "Good morning." A rumble of salutations was returned. "I thought it was about time I introduced myself. I'm Skyler Ridge." Then he cleared his throat, pushing away his stage name. "Actually, my real name is Skyler Clark, and you're welcome to call me Sky." Everyone stared as though they were looking at a mirage, so Skyler went straight to the reason he was here. "I'm guessing you all know about the story in *Stars Today*, and I wanted to clear the air. What they reported is not true. Well, most of it. I did just move to Maple Bay, but Myra and I are not dating. The tabloids like to make up their own stories about what I'm up to and, unfortunately, Myra got thrown into their nonsense."

The stares continued. He thought he heard a cricket, and Skyler wondered if this was the best way to approach this. Maybe he should've talked to Myra first.

A bell cut the silence. An actual *clanging* bell.

Skyler looked for the source of the unexpected clatter and found Myra. She was behind the counter, next to the register. Her hand was raised, and she was rattling a . . . *cowbell*? Myra held the metal instrument above her head and clanged it until she had the attention of everyone in the shop.

Myra set the noisemaker down next to the cash register. "I think we might have forgotten our manners. It doesn't matter what was said in some silly magazine. What matters is that Skyler is new to our community, and he deserves a warm welcome. He's a person. Not a story. And as long as I've got a captive audience, I'd like to introduce you all to my new business partner, Mr. Clark." Heads swiveled between Myra and Skyler. "So, what do you say we give Skyler a warm Maple Bay welcome? Because you'll be seeing a lot more of him around here."

The silence held for a few more seconds. Then it broke like a cracked dam. The impromptu meet-and-greet started with a trickle and turned into a rush of introductions.

A spry group of elderly women approached. "Mighty nice to finally meet you," the woman in the front said. "I'm Eleanor. This is Patty and Kandi. We were here last week when Myra sprinkled you with a smoothie." Eleanor smirked with a twinkle in her eye. "Been wanting to meet you ever since."

"It was a little more than a sprinkle," Patty said.

Kandi chuckled. "More like a shower."

"Lovely to meet you." Skyler smiled and shook each of their hands. "And I'd like you to know Myra hasn't doused me in anything since."

The ladies laughed.

"Well, that's good to hear," Eleanor said. "Welcome to Maple Bay."

"Thank you."

Right behind the ladies, a man that looked to be in his eighties approached. He wore a corduroy flat cap and walked with a cane. "Vernon Richards." He reached out and shook Skyler's hand. His grip was stronger than Skyler had expected. "I'm Myra's grandpa, and I'm glad you decided to come into town this morning." He put his hand near his mouth like he had a secret. "Judy told me about you, and I wasn't sure how long I could keep the information to myself." He winked.

Skyler grinned. "Nice to meet you, sir. And thanks for keeping my secret."

"Looking forward to getting to know you," Vernon said. "Any friend of my granddaughter's is a friend of mine."

Making his way through the crowd, Skyler met a slice of Maple Bay—each person greeting him with excitement. It wasn't the welcome he'd expected. Instead of treating him like a washed-up imposter, he was being greeted like the town mayor. By the time he made it over to Myra, the people in the shop were talking among themselves, enjoying each other's' company. There was less gawking, and no one was taking pictures.

Skyler stepped behind the counter and gave Myra a smile. "Hey."

"Hey, Mr. Clark."

"You can call me Sky."

She hooked a thumb in her apron pocket and grinned. "One step at a time, Mr. Clark."

The tension in Skyler's chest waned. "You're pretty handy with that cowbell."

"I usually use it to hold down the stack of napkins, but it definitely got everyone's attention. I should try it on my kids sometime."

He laughed but grew serious as he stepped closer. "I didn't look at my phone until this morning. I had no idea the story came out yesterday, but I wanted you to know I'm sorry you got pulled into that stupid article. I didn't realize anyone was taking pictures of us. That can be a hazard of hanging around me."

She suddenly looked uncomfortable and flicked a hand like she was dismissing the issue. "It's not your fault. Don't worry about it."

"I can't promise it won't happen again."

She shook her head. "I can handle myself. If anyone wants the truth, I'll give it to them. Besides, the story gave Perkup a big boost in sales, so there's a silver lining. We've been packed all morning."

Skyler looked around. Everyone had a mug in their hand. Becca was taking orders from a long line at the register.

"Need help?" he asked. "I can run the whipped cream."

That made her smile. "Grab an apron."

Chapter Thirteen

Myra knocked on Skyler's front door. Her chest tightened when he opened it. Skyler was wearing a black T-shirt and dark jeans. The same outfit he'd worn a few hours earlier—under an apron.

"Myra?" The surprise on his face pushed her to show him why she was here.

She raised her hand. "You forgot your phone at the shop."

"Oh, thanks." He opened the screen door and stepped out.

"You're not very good at keeping track of this thing." She handed him the device.

"Actually, I'm not particularly fond of it. A lot of my headaches go away when I ignore it." Skyler slid the phone into his back pocket. "But thanks for dropping it off. You didn't have to do that."

"No problem. The kids and I were just running some errands. We're off to the grocery store to pick up stuff for dinner. Didn't mean to interrupt."

Dishes clinked from inside the house.

Skyler looked over Myra's shoulder and waved.

"Hey, Sky!" Finch yelled from the truck.

Myra glanced back. Her son was waving ferociously out the open window. Paisley waved too, but with the calmness of an embarrassed teenager.

"Why don't you guys join us for dinner?" Skyler asked, jerking Myra's attention back to him. "Carol made a whole spread. Way more than Grandma and I can eat."

"What? Oh, no. We couldn't." Myra stumbled through her words. She had groceries to get. Laundry to do. Horses to feed. Besides, she was a mess. After she'd finished at the shop, she'd thrown on an old T-shirt and barn jeans that had toured the stables all week without hitting the washing machine. "We shouldn't. I've got so much to do, and I'm feeding the horses tonight."

"What time? I mean, I know they get fed before the sun's up, due to your call the other morning." A corner of his mouth rose. "But when do you feed them at night?"

"Six or seven, usually."

"Then you've got time. It's barely five. We eat early around here. That way, you don't have to go get groceries or make dinner. You can check two errands off your list."

"Oh . . ." Myra's brain short-circuited at the thought. It would be awfully nice not to have to cook for once. In fact, she wasn't even planning to actually cook this evening. It was a grab-a-frozen-piz-za-at-the-store kind of night. The busy day at the shop had worn her out.

"Carol made fried chicken, and I promise you don't want to miss it," he added.

Dinner with Skyler was tempting, but Myra had plenty of reasons to pass. First, he was handsome enough to make a nun blush, and she didn't want to explore the effect he had on her. Second, Myra was discovering she enjoyed his company. Skyler was a genuinely nice person, and the more she got to know him, the more guilt she felt for her agreement with Cedric. But before she could come up with another excuse to pass on dinner, Skyler shouted out to the kids.

"Hey, Finchy?" Skyler called. Her son was still hanging out the window. "You and Paisley want to join me for dinner? You like fried chicken, mashed potatoes, creamed corn, and chocolate pie?"

Finch pushed the truck door open a millisecond after Skyler mentioned fried chicken. By the time Skyler said *chocolate pie*, his boots were on the ground.

"Yes, sir!" Finch ran toward the house, leaving the truck door wide open. Paisley scooted out as well, shaking her head at her brother.

Myra laughed as Finch ran up onto the deck. "Looks like we're staying for dinner."

Skyler opened the screen door with a smile. Myra and her crew entered.

A half hour later, Myra was stuffed to the gills. She considered unclasping the top button of her jeans but decided her comfort could wait. As it was, she was sporting barn clothes at a dining room table that definitely cost more than her truck. She didn't need another reason to look like she had no manners. But despite her thoughts, Skyler hadn't made her feel inadequate. Not in the least. The lacquered ten-person table was set with fine china and decorated with a beautiful bouquet of lilies, but Myra got the feeling the formality of dinner was more for Dorthea than for Skyler.

Dorthea sat across the table from Myra, looking cute as a button. Her white hair was coifed and her makeup done, as though she'd expected guests. She wore a pastel sweater and slacks. Skyler seemed at ease in his T-shirt and jeans. He put his elbows on the table and had only used one of the forks in the place setting. Myra appreciated his casual approach, and it didn't seem as though she or her kids had offended Dorthea with their lack of etiquette. Dorthea had been all smiles throughout the dinner, asking the kids questions and laughing at their stories.

"That was delicious," Finch said to Carol as she reached past him to take his dessert plate away. "Thank you."

"You are very welcome." Carol grinned from ear to ear.

"Doesn't she make the best chocolate pie?" Dorthea asked, and the table groaned in agreement.

"Seriously, if you're willing to give out your recipe, I'll gladly take it." Myra licked her lips. She thought about licking her plate, but she'd swiped up every last crumb and chocolate smear with her fork. Plus, there was the manners thing, again. "That pie would be a hit at Sunday supper."

Paisley nodded in agreement. "It sure would." She'd also cleaned her plate.

"I don't give out my recipes easily, but any friend of Skyler and Dorthea's is a friend of mine. I'll write it down for you." Carol gathered Paisley's plate.

Myra rose from her chair. "Are you sure I can't help you?"

"No, child. Sit. Enjoy. Relax. This is my job, and I can't have you encroaching on my responsibilities." Carol gave Myra a good-natured wink. Still, Myra felt funny about letting someone wait on her. Even if it was Carol's job.

"Thank you for another amazing dinner, Carol," Skyler said, sitting back in his chair.

"I'm so glad you all could join us." Dorthea's eyes sparkled, and Myra was glad Skyler had pushed for her and her kids to stay. They clearly weren't intruding. Dorthea had obviously enjoyed their company. Especially that of the kids.

"Before we leave, can you play your guitar for us?" Finch asked, out of nowhere.

Myra's first reaction was to tell Finch that they needed to get going. She didn't want Skyler to feel like he had to put on a show.

Before she could speak, Dorthea chimed in. "Oh, of course he can. My Sky would love to share his talent with you all." Dorthea beamed, and Myra zipped her lips. She was not about to contradict Skyler's grandma.

Besides, Skyler didn't look put out by Finch's request. "Sure." He stood from his chair and gathered an acoustic guitar from the corner of the kitchen. It had been sitting there like a house plant. "What would you like me to play?" Instead of returning to the head of the table, Skyler walked over and pulled out the chair next to Finch.

Finch scooted his chair back to get a better view of Skyler. "You know that one song you sing about trucks and dirt roads?"

Skyler situated the golden guitar on his lap and chuckled. "Yeah, I know that one."

Paisley leaned on the table, peering around her brother. "Skyler uses an electric guitar for that one, Finch. How about 'This Should've Been a Love Song'?"

Myra knew the song Paisley was referring to. It had been a huge hit a decade ago, and Myra was surprised that Paisley knew of it. She'd been four or five when it was popular. The song was beautiful and deep, and Myra was sure Skyler's husky voice would do the lyrics justice. But it wasn't Skyler's song. It had been sung by a well-known husband-and-wife duo—The Heartmakers—and told a story of a love that never was.

Skyler looked intrigued by Paisley's request. "It's been a long time since I've sung that one."

"You wrote it, right?" Paisley asked, looking proud of her tidbit of information. Had her daughter been doing a little research of her own?

"I did." Skyler situated his fingers on the guitar and strummed a chord.

"Cool." Paisley tilted her head. "I thought so."

Myra wasn't sure which surprised her more, Paisley softening her too-cool-for-everything teenage defiance, or the idea that Skyler had written a song that had made Myra cry—many times.

"Oh, that's one of my favorites." Dorthea put her elbows on the edge of the table and clasped her hands together. "Yes, please play that one."

Paisley grinned widely, showing off her braces and the adorable smile Myra wished she saw more of.

For a moment, Skyler stared at his hand. It cupped the neck of the guitar, and Myra wondered what had captured his thoughts. Did he not want to sing? Did the song remind him of someone he'd lost? But as his fingers found the strings, he breathed life into his guitar and filled the house with music. He sang verses about losing a love he'd never had, and Myra found herself lost in his words—in the tone of his voice, the emotion that captured his face, and a story that was hidden somewhere behind his amber eyes. Skyler portrayed the song better with his single voice than The Heartmakers had with their harmonies.

As he neared the end of the song, Myra's throat tightened. Her heart broke. She felt the story Skyler was telling. His voice traveled across the table and hit her in the chest, forcing her eyes to well. And when he strung the last few notes, a single tear escaped her. She meant to wipe it away before anyone saw, but Skyler blinked himself out of the song, and his gaze clicked to hers. As the last note hung in the air, he watched a tear slide over Myra's cheek. She wiped it away with her fingertips.

"Such a beautiful song," Dorthea said, breaking their gaze.

Myra gave her cheek one more swipe, making sure to erase the evidence of the tear. "It really is."

"That's great and all," Finch addressed the table before turning back to Skyler. "But can you sing the one about trucks and dirt roads now? Instead of a sappy one?"

A laugh bubbled out of Myra. Paisley shook her head at her brother but laughed as well.

"For you, I will," Skyler said to Finch, looking amused. "The acoustic version."

Finch wiggled to sit up straight, now thoroughly engrossed in the song choice. But even as Skyler sang about diesel and dust, Myra couldn't get the last song out of her head. How he'd grabbed her heart with the intensity of his voice. The emotion that had hung on each word. Verses he'd written. But when Skyler finished singing, he managed to hit her in the heart again as he took the time to show each of her kids how to play a few chords on his guitar. Myra couldn't get past the way he made Finch and Paisley smile, and her heart swelled for an entirely different reason.

Chapter Fourteen

The rest of the week felt different. Unexpected and easy. Like Skyler had taken a wrong turn and accidentally found a scenic route. Maybe it was being away from the chaos of his usual life, or maybe it was how Maple Bay had accepted him since Myra had set the town straight. Maybe it was all the time he'd been able to spend with his grandma? Seeing her smile, knowing firsthand that she was having more good days than tough ones. Regardless, Skyler knew the change in his outlook had been pushed along by the bold cowgirl who'd landed unwillingly in his life.

He glanced over at that cowgirl now. Myra was standing in front of the espresso machine. Her apron covered a black tank top and dark jeans. Her black hair was twirled into a twist and held in place with a few pencils, which seemed like a magic trick to Skyler. He kept wanting to pull the pencils out and watch her hair spill down her back.

Myra looked over and gave him a soft smile. He'd seen more of those this week. "Looks like Mom's table might need some refills," she said while clicking a portafilter into the espresso machine, prepping to pull a shot.

"I got it." Skyler slid behind her, resisting the urge to place his hand on Myra's lower back. Instead, he grabbed a carafe of coffee and walked to the table by the front window. Judy, Joyce, and Eleanor were engrossed in a conversation about quilts. Finch and Paisley also sat at the table. It was Friday, and school had let out early for teachers' conferences. However, the kids didn't look impressed by the quilt conversation. "Anyone need more coffee?"

"Yes, please," Judy said and slid her mug toward Skyler. He started pouring. "Just a half cup though."

"Me too," Judy's sister, Joyce, added with a friendly smile.

As Skyler topped off their mugs, Eleanor raved about the black-berry-maple latte. "I didn't think anything would take me away from my peppermint mochas, but the new special is just to die for."

"That's all Myra," Skyler said. "She came up with that combination."

"It sounds weird." Finch squinted from the end of the table.

Paisley looked up from her phone. "Not any weirder than those soda bombs you make." Paisley hooked her thumb toward her brother. "He likes to combine root beer, orange pop, and cherry 7-Up."

Finch shrugged. "What? It's good."

Eleanor and Paisley made faces of disgust.

"I'm not so sure about that, Finch." Skyler laughed. "But I'll take your word for it."

Finch smiled. "Don't knock it until you try it!"

All week, Skyler had been coming into Perkup for a few hours here and there, learning the business. Myra was teaching him how to make drinks and how she ran the shop. She introduced him to customers, and Skyler was pleasantly surprised to find the regulars treated him like a normal person—which was something he hadn't realized he was craving. It was a stark contrast to how he was used to being treated. And he appreciated that. Today, Skyler had been at the shop since opening. Becca had the day off, and even though Myra told Skyler she could handle the shop herself, he'd insisted on helping. Actually, he'd been looking forward to his time in the shop. And his time with Myra.

From the back of the shop, Myra laughed, grabbing Skyler's attention. She was talking with a few women in the corner booth. He didn't know what they were talking about, but he couldn't ignore Myra's laughter. It was like his favorite bourbon—smooth and guaranteed to lighten his mind. Which was why he felt cheated when a man entered through the back hall and cut Myra's laughter short.

"Daddy!" Finch yelled before running across the shop.

"Hey, buddy," the man replied. Finch launched himself into his arms. Paisley followed, also draping her dad in a hug.

"Look who decided to show up," Judy said under her breath.

Skyler wasn't sure he was supposed to have heard her comment, but Judy's tone put him on edge. Skyler walked to the next table and filled more mugs, though his ears strained to hear the conversation Myra was having with her ex-husband. Her arms were crossed over her chest. Her face was neutral, and she was nodding. Soon, Myra gave Finch and Paisley each a kiss on the cheek, and they left with their father.

Myra retreated behind the counter and filled a blender with the ingredients for a blended iced coffee. When Skyler joined her, she turned on the appliance. Skyler waited for the loud whirling to end.

"Hey, you okay?" he asked.

Myra set out a plastic cup. "Yeah, I'm fine." She didn't look at him.

"You sure?" Skyler was tiptoeing into uncharted territory, but he pressed on. "'Cause you don't seem fine."

She shook the icy drink out of the blender. When the last of it filled the cup, she said, "That was the kids' father, Luis. He loves to pop in when it's convenient for him." Her forehead wrinkled in what Skyler assumed was frustration. "I was going to take the kids to a movie at the drive-in tonight, but Luis surprised them with tickets for an indoor amusement park over in Brainerd." Before Skyler could reply, she shook her head like she was done with the topic. "It's fine. They'll have fun. It's not about that. I just—"

The bell on the front door jingled, and a couple walked in. Myra took a breath and gave Skyler a barely there smile. As she walked past Skyler to greet the customers, she gave him a squeeze on the arm. He wasn't sure if it was a silent thank you or a plea to end the conversation, but they never did circle back. Myra stayed busy until Skyler headed out.

Later that night, Skyler was still thinking of Myra, wishing he'd asked more, wanting to make sure she was all right. Was she sitting home alone when she wanted to be with her kids?

As the sun set, Skyler decided to go for a spin. He picked up a bouquet of flowers, wanting to brighten Myra's day, but as he drove down Main Street and Perkup came into view, he frowned at the shop's windows. The red barn was completely dark. Disappointment settled in his chest, but what had he been hoping for? For Myra to greet him with a big smile? For a little alone time with her? *Yes and yes.*

Maybe it was a good thing she wasn't home.

Deciding to stop in and leave the flowers in the shop, Skyler pulled into the back alley. As he did, his headlights landed on Myra. She was walking across the alley, dressed in a hot-pink bathrobe. A towel was twirled around her head, and a glass of wine teetered in her fingers. Suddenly she froze like her poofy pink slippers were glued to the gravel. Skyler thought she also dropped a few cuss words, but he could only read her lips.

Skyler stifled laughter. He put his car in park and turned off the headlights, taking Myra out of the spotlight. He opened his door and got out.

"I like the slippers," he said, resting his arm on the top of the open car door. Truthfully, he liked the whole outfit.

"Oh, for cripes' sake," Myra said into the dark, though Skyler still had a pretty good view of her. Judy's porch light shone into the alley. Plus, the hot-pink bathrobe practically glowed in the dark. "Well, this is embarrassing."

"Embarrassing? Why?"

"I feel like I don't have to explain that one. I'm standing in the alley in my bathrobe."

Skyler couldn't stop a chuckle. "Can I ask what you're doing? I mean, you don't have to tell me if you don't want. It really isn't my business."

Myra shuffled over, stopping at the hood of his car. "It's Friday. I needed a glass of wine and a bubble bath."

Skyler thrummed his fingers against the door. "And you ended up outside *how?*"

She took a sip of wine before answering. "There isn't a bathtub in my place. Just a shower. So I use Mom's when I need a soak."

"Oh. That makes sense."

This time, Myra laughed. "You say that like it's normal to find a woman lurking through the dark like this." She waved a hand up and down her body. "You're a big celebrity. I bet you've found women lurking outside your house before. Must be nice to finally find a woman creeping around her own place for once." She flashed a grin at him.

Skyler chuckled, finding himself fascinated by how she rolled with the punches and gave as good as she got. "Actually, it is."

"And might I ask what you're doing here? Isn't it like eight o'clock?"

"It is." A flutter rolled through his stomach. Was it weird that he'd brought her flowers? "I wanted to stop by and give you these."

He reached inside his car and pulled out the dozen yellow roses. They were wrapped in white paper and tied with a string of burlap. He'd picked them up at the market on the way over. When Myra's eyes landed on the flowers, Skyler wondered if he should've checked in with her via text instead. Her mouth hung open.

"You got those for me?" she asked after a few awkward beats.

"It seemed like you were upset after your kids left today. I thought these would cheer you up." He closed his car door and stepped toward Myra, handing her the bouquet.

"Oh, wow. Thank you." She took the flowers. "I don't know what to say."

She looked uncomfortable, so Skyler added, "My grandma loves roses and always said yellow roses were a symbol of friendship." Dorthea had included Skyler on many conversations concerning the flower. "Although now that I've seen your robe, maybe I should've gotten you pink."

The unease slipped from Myra's face. It was replaced by a cheeky smile. "I love roses too." She tipped the bouquet toward her and took a deep breath, closing her eyes. Skyler watched unabashedly until her eyelids fluttered open. "Friendship, huh?"

"Friends." No question mark. Though he might've added an ellipsis. They could've been more than friends if they'd met under different circumstances, but being friends was a lot better than where they'd started off. A whole lot better. "I mean, now that you've stopped looking at me like you might run me over, I think we can be friends. Don't you?"

She grinned at his sarcasm. "Yeah, I do." She laid the bouquet in her arm like it was a baby, careful not to bump the wineglass in her hand. "And I'll try not to give you the evil eye anymore. Sometimes it just happens though. I can't always control what my face does."

Skyler liked that about her. Most people told him what they thought he wanted to hear. But Myra said what she thought.

"So, now that you don't have the kids tonight, what are you up to?" He didn't want to be too forward and invite himself in. He owned the building, but Myra lived there, and he'd respect her space. Still, there was a part of him that wanted to ask her out for a drink or a walk along the lake.

"What am I up to? You're looking at it." She huffed, raising her wineglass again. "Geez, it's eight o'clock on a Friday night, and the only other thing I have planned is curling up in bed and watching an episode of *Dateline*. I used to be fun. I swear." She shook her head at herself. "I don't know when I turned into an old lady."

Skyler thought Myra was plenty fun, but it sounded like she needed a reminder of that. "Maybe we could do something together?"

She pursed her lips. "What did you have in mind?"

"What's something you used to do . . . back when you were 'fun'?" Skyler made air quotes with his fingers. "Something that made you high on life. Something you haven't done in forever." He was truly curious what was going to come out of Myra's mouth, especially since it looked like she was perusing files in her head.

"Well . . ." She transferred her wineglass to her free hand and took a sip. "My cousins and I used to climb the water tower."

That, he hadn't been expecting. "Is that a thing? You can climb water towers?"

"Sure. I mean, you're not supposed to, but the view from the top is amazing, especially at night. You can see the whole town. Used to do it a lot in high school. It was this secret space my cousins and I shared that made us feel invincible, like the world was ours for the taking." She played with the burlap string tied around the flowers. The memory had sparked something in her eyes. "That's silly, though. That's something I did as a kid. I can't believe I just suggested we—"

"Let's do it."

Myra's mouth gaped. "Really?"

He stepped forward and reached out for the bouquet. "I'll put the roses in a vase while you change into something other than a bathrobe and slippers. You can watch *Dateline* another night."

Chapter Fifteen

Myra climbed the metal ladder on the side of the water tower, edging closer to the night sky with every rung. When she was a stone's throw from the deck that wrapped the cylinder tank, she glanced down. Which was a *very* bad idea. Skyler was just below her, perched on the ladder, but she barely saw him. Instantly, she realized how far they were from the ground.

"You okay?" he asked, and Myra's gaze flicked to his.

"I . . ." she started, gripping the metal rung tightly. When she'd changed out of her pajamas and bathrobe, she'd thrown on cutoff shorts, a light sweater, and cowboy boots. She hadn't given much thought to her shoe choice. She used to run up this ladder in flip-flops, but now she wished she'd grabbed a pair of tennis shoes. Something with a secure grip. "I'm starting to wonder if this was a good idea." She also wondered when she'd lost her youth and invincibility.

"Look up," Skyler said, and she tilted her head to the sky. Once she did, the panic eased. "Is that better? Or do you want to go back down?"

"Better." Myra took a deep breath and forced it from her lungs. She was five or six rungs from the deck. She could practically grab it. "We're almost there. I think I'm okay now."

"I'm right behind you."

Myra pushed forward and finagled the last bit of the ladder, thankful to place her hands and knees on the deck. She crawled away from the ladder, giving Skyler room to join her. They both settled with their butts on the deck and their backs pressed against the big tank. Myra turned her head toward Skyler. Their eyes met, and nervous laughter bubbled out of them both.

"I don't remember that being so scary." Myra shook her head.

"It is a long way up." Skyler's jean-clad legs stretched out before him, covering the width of the deck. His boots reached the flimsy railing, but the fact that he was also wearing cowboy boots somehow made Myra feel better.

"It *is* a long way up," she replied. They went quiet, taking in the twinkling view of Maple Bay. The water tower loomed over the edge of town. It oversaw rooftops, streetlamps, and the shimmering dark blue of the lake. The sight was an elixir for her nerves.

"You came up here as a kid?"

"When I was a teenager." Myra blinked, remembering. "It started as a dare after a Friday-night football game. My cousins and I were cruising Main Street with friends, but you can only drive up and down three blocks of Main Street so many times. We got bored."

Skyer grinned, amused. "Yeah, I suppose."

"I think it was my cousin Evan that proposed the dare. Evan and Jesse always tried to one-up each other, and pretty soon, they were both racing to the top of the water tower. Our buddy Creed went too. My cousin Kat and I weren't about to miss out, so we climbed up as well. Then it became a ritual. After each hometown football game, we'd all come up here. Small-town fun, I guess." She shrugged, but the memory warmed her heart. "What about you? What kind of trouble did you get into as a kid? No water towers in Nashville?"

"There are water towers in Nashville. I just never thought of climbing them. But I can see I missed out." He stared off into the starry sky, and Myra examined his strong profile. His chiseled jaw. His Adam's apple as he swallowed. "Besides, I mostly grew up in Los Angeles. And I got in plenty of trouble without the temptation of water towers."

"How so?" Myra pulled her bare knees to her chest and wrapped her arms around them.

"Drinking. Partying. I lost my mom when I was young, and I'm not sure my dad ever wanted to be a parent. He wasn't around much."

"I'm sorry."

"Don't be." He slid one foot back, angling his leg in front of his chest. "His absence gave me much-needed time in Nashville with my grandparents. They're really who raised me. My dad remarried a few years after Mom passed, and he was always off exploring some beach or foreign country with his new wife. I spent every holiday, spring break, and summer with my grandma and grandpa."

Myra's heart swelled and broke in the same instant. Her parents had divorced when she was a teenager, and her relationship with her father was strained, but she'd always been close with her mother, even though they could butt heads with the best of them. Plus, her circle of family was tight. She had an array of aunts, uncles, and cousins that had always been a part of her life. "I'm glad you had your grandparents."

"Me too." He nodded. "Not sure what I would've done without them."

"No brothers or sisters?" she asked quietly.

"No. Just me." His fingertips brushed aimlessly over his pant leg, and Myra imagined how Dorthea's memory loss must be impacting him. Grandmothers were special, irreplaceable, but Dorthea was more than a grandmother to Skyler.

"I really enjoyed having dinner with you and Dorthea the other night. The kids did too," Myra said truthfully. "And it wasn't just because I didn't have to cook or clean up." Myra's comment earned a smirk from Skyler. "Your grandma is really sweet."

Skyler tipped his head. "Sweet. Dependable. Sassy. Actually, you remind me a lot of her."

She pursed her lips at him. "Was that a compliment or did you just call me old?"

"It was a compliment." He laughed. "You're a great mother."

His unexpected praise startled her. He'd brought her roses *and* complimented the title closest to her heart? If he was trying to win points with her, he'd accomplished that tonight.

"Thank you," Myra replied. "Sometimes I'm not sure I'm doing the whole parenting thing right. So it's really nice to hear that."

"I think you've got it right. You're raising two great kids. I really enjoyed showing them how to play guitar the other night."

"Oh, they loved that. Neither one has stopped talking about it. Paisley even hinted that she'd like to take lessons now."

"I'd be happy to give her lessons. Finch too, if he's interested. I've got plenty of guitars if they'd like something to practice on. I could bring a couple to the shop?"

The sweetness of Skyler's offer touched Myra. It kind of blew her mind that he'd offer to give her kids lessons. "They'd love that."

Skyler smiled at her. "My grandma is actually the one that got me into music."

"She did?"

"Yeah. She's been playing piano since she was a kid. Used to play for her church choir. I remember watching her every Sunday when I stayed with my grandparents. I didn't necessarily like going to church, but listening to Grandma play distracted me from the uncertainty of my life. She played at home too. Sometimes I'd play with her. And when I turned into a handful of a teenager, she put a guitar in my hands. Got me some lessons. It gave me direction. Something to focus on and pour my feelings into. Music became my safety net. Since then, it's been a safe place to land, even when times are tough. Maybe especially then."

Myra's breathing slowed. "I get that. Horses are that for me. Always a refuge when life is rough." Her mind flitted back to the song Skyler had sung after dinner the other night. How the words and melody had moved her to tears. "When did you start writing songs?"

"Not long after I started playing guitar."

"Did you always write country songs?"

Skyler nodded. "My grandparents played a lot of country music when I was a kid. They played all the greats on an old record player. I found myself lost in the stories those singers told. The strong sense of home in their songs. Country music was like a balm for my soul. It never left me. It's always been what I wanted to sing."

Myra stared at Skyler, processing his words—which made sense and confused her at the same time. "Why don't you just come out and say that? Tell your truth to the press? That you sing country music because of how it makes you *feel*. Because you connect to it. Not because of where you came from or how you live your life."

He looked off, over the town lights. "I guess I just don't want to explain myself anymore. I'm over—" A low roll of thunder groaned in the distance, cutting him off.

Myra shifted and assessed the inky blue sky. "We should probably get going. This isn't the place to be during a storm." She didn't want to end their conversation, but sitting on a metal tower as lightning rolled in was not a good idea. Maybe they could talk more at her place?

Myra braced herself, gathering the courage to stand, but Skyler beat her to it. He got to his feet and reached for her. She placed both hands in his, and he helped her up. Standing directly in front of Skyler, looking up into his eyes, Myra's heart lurched. She nervously sputtered the first thing that came to mind. "Do *not* tell my kids we did this. I don't want them getting any crazy ideas."

A grin slid across his lips. "Don't want them doing what you did as a kid?"

"No. Absolutely not," she said with all seriousness. "Now that I have my own kids, I understand what my mom was talking about. I must've given her about a million heart attacks over the years. I definitely don't need my kids following in my footsteps."

"You're being too hard on yourself. Those footsteps got you here. They made you who you are." The gaze that came with his words circled around her like a tornado, threatening to pull her in and spin her about.

With their hands still clasped together, Myra thought about the yellow roses. About how Skyler had asked for her friendship only an hour earlier. But the growing electricity between them felt unlike any friendship she'd ever had. She started to ask him about the roses, wanting to pry deeper into why he'd stopped by, but a flash of lightning lit the sky, and Myra gasped. The bright flash, combined with the knowledge that she was high above the ground, instantly made her dizzy. She wobbled. Skyler grabbed her so quickly that she barely understood what was happening until her back was pressed against the metal tank.

"Hey," he breathed, grabbing her attention. Skyler had her by the shoulders. His grip was strong, steady. He stood between her and the night sky like he'd protect her from the storm. She thought she'd let him. "You all right?"

For a few pounding heartbeats, she considered his question. *Am I?*

Skyler's touch. His searching eyes. His overpowering presence. All of it tempted her. She wanted to push past her nerves, take a risk, and discover what she'd find at the top of this tower.

"I'm okay," she reassured him. Then her fingers found his shirt and wrapped into the soft cotton. She gave a gentle tug. Skyler closed the gap between them.

He lowered his mouth to hers, brushing her lips gently but keeping a steady grip on her shoulders, not letting her back leave the safety of the tank. When he deepened the kiss, Myra's insides melted. Her heartbeat echoed throughout her entire body. Skyler might've felt it in her lips.

His kiss burned through her. It exhausted her defenses. She felt desired, something she hadn't felt since who knew when.

When Skyler eased back and traced a line of kisses along her jaw and down her neck, Myra closed her eyes, taking in his whisper-soft touch. The heat of his breath danced across her neck, and when his lips pressed to the sensitive skin just below her ear, Myra thought she imagined another roll of thunder . . . until it cracked loudly through the air, like the end of a whip.

She jerked, but Skyler maintained a strong grip on her shoulders. His lips found hers again, and Myra was certain she was melting down the side of the tower. Before she could disintegrate, lightning flashed. Skyler pulled back, and Myra realized her hands were fisted in his shirt, pulling it taut across his chest. With help from the illuminated sky, she watched his copper eyes smolder.

"We should get down from here," Myra said through a heavy breath. She wasn't sure if she was referring to the water tower or the high they'd just discovered.

Skyler kissed her again before they broke apart and started down the ladder.

Chapter Sixteen

Skyler climbed down the ladder first, which might've been a bad idea, because he kept looking up at Myra. He hadn't known cowboy boots could be so sexy. The boots combined with Myra's curvy legs and cutoff shorts nearly made him fall to his doom, multiple times. He'd admired Myra on the way up, but after kissing her, the sight was almost too much to handle.

By the time she joined him on the ground, raindrops were plunking down from the dark. Myra gave a playful screech, throwing an arm in the air like it might serve as an umbrella. Skyler grabbed her hand, and they ran for his car, squealing like a couple of kids. The rain came harder. When they reached the passenger door, Skyler jerked it open, and Myra ducked in. He ran to the driver's side and jumped in as well. When his door slammed shut, Myra set her head back on the headrest and belly laughed. He wasn't sure there was a sweeter sound than the pelting rain and her happiness.

"Well, that was *fun*," Myra said, tilting her head toward him. "A lot more fun than an episode of *Dateline*."

"A lot more." He blew out a laugh. "Thanks for my first water tower adventure."

"My pleasure."

Pleasure. What an appropriate word.

Skyler should've fired up his car and taken Myra home, but he couldn't resist one more kiss. He leaned over and slid his hand against her now-wet neck. His fingers weaved into loose, damp hair. The rain had given them both a good soaking. Somehow, it also made the scent of Myra's freshly bathed skin even more apparent. She smelled like sugar and cinnamon. Sweet with a kick of spice. The smell fit her to a tee.

Skyler kissed away a raindrop on her cheek before meeting her lips and losing himself in Myra once again. His heart thudded like the first time he'd stepped on stage, but there was more to kissing Myra than the way she made his heart race. Around her, Skyler felt seen. She looked past his fame, money, and even what the tabloids spewed about him. She was the first person in a long time who'd done that.

Myra returned his kiss. For a minute, pure, heated bliss filled the car. Then she pulled back.

Skyler was cradling her head. His fingers fell from her tresses, and he was about to ask if something was wrong when Myra said, "I need to ask you something."

He stared at her, hazy with want. "Of course. Ask me anything."

"Do you—" she started, but her phone interrupted with a loud ring. Myra's phone was on the dash, and the glowing screen lit the interior of the car. Skyler saw Paisley's name. It was nearly eleven o'clock, so Skyler wasn't surprised when Myra lurched forward and grabbed her phone.

"Paisley?" she answered, pressing the phone to her ear. "Everything okay?"

Skyler assumed Paisley and Finch were still with their dad, but Myra's tone suggested it was not normal for her daughter to call at this hour. He sat back, watching and listening.

"Does he have a fever?" Myra asked. "That doesn't sound good. Yes, of course. I'll be there shortly." She ended the call and looked at Skyler. "I'm sorry. Finch is sick, and he wants me to pick him up. Paisley said she's not feeling great either."

"They're at their dad's?"

Myra nodded. "Finch has always been a bit of a momma's boy." She smiled softly, reveling in the fact. "He likes how I take care of him when he doesn't feel good. Says his dad's not as good at it."

Skyler figured Myra was the kind of mom who would pull out all the stops when her kids were sick. She doted on them on a normal day. "Where does their dad live? I can take you."

Her forehead wrinkled. "Finch has been puking. I'd feel really bad if he puked in your car."

"Well, I'd feel really bad if I kept you from getting to him quickly." He started the car. "Tell me where to go."

"Okay. Thank you." Myra clicked her seatbelt into place and rattled off directions. A few turns and one stop sign later, Skyler parked in front of a one-level ranch-style house. In the quiet neighborhood, it was the only house with lights on. He caught movement in a front window.

"I'll be right back." Myra got out of the car and jogged to the front door. She went right in.

Skyler stepped out of his car, not sure what to do, but he wanted to help. A few minutes later, Myra came out the front door. She was carrying Finch—one hand on his back, the other under his rump. The poor kid's arms were wrapped around her shoulders.

Skyler walked toward them, wanting to take Finch from her. Myra was strong—Skyler had no doubt of that—but Finch was a lanky ten-year-old. He stood almost to her shoulder. Why wasn't his dad carrying him?

Nearly to the stoop, Skyler said, "Here, let me help you. I can carry Finch."

Myra looked a bit stunned. "It's okay. I've got him."

Paisley was just behind her, wearing sweats and flip-flops. She looked tired, but not as sickly as Finch.

"Hey, Sky," Finch grumbled without lifting his head. Myra turned so her son could see Skyler. "Whatcha doing?" He was pale as a ghost, his cheek smashed against Myra's shoulder. Finch lifted his lips at the corners like he hadn't just been puking.

"Coming to pick you up. You not feeling so good?" Skyler asked.

"Nah."

Paisley stepped onto the stairs. "He threw up all the cotton candy he ate. It was blue. So was his puke."

"Well, I'm going to give you guys a ride home." Skyler looked at Myra. "Are you sure you don't want me to take him?"

"No, it's okay. Your car's not far," she said, just as the kids' father appeared behind Paisley. He carried a small duffel bag. When his gaze landed on Skyler, he looked thoroughly confused.

"Luis, this is Skyler." Myra barely turned back to look at him. Granted, she was holding a kid.

"The guitar guy," Finch added.

"The singer," Paisley corrected her brother.

"Hey," Luis replied. Confusion hadn't left his face, but Skyler figured Luis already knew who he was. The kids, Myra, or just about anyone in town might have told him. Not to mention, he'd probably seen the pictures in the press earlier this week.

"Nice to meet you. I'm the new partner." Skyler offered his hand. Luis gave him a funny look. "At Perkup," Skyler added, realizing how his introduction had sounded. Luis was probably wondering why Skyler and Myra were together at this time of night.

"Nice to meet you." Luis shook his hand. Then he focused on Myra. "I thought it was a mix of the carnival food and rollercoasters, but then he spiked a fever." Luis and Myra shared a few more pieces of information, and then they walked to Skyler's car as a group. Myra eased Finch into the backseat. Paisley took the duffel bag from her dad and joined Finch.

When Skyler pulled away from the house, Luis was walking back toward the open front door. A woman was waiting for him. She gave a wave, looking out of place. No one mentioned who she was. Skyler didn't ask. He just got them home.

The next morning, Skyler rose before dawn and opened the coffee shop. By himself. He brewed coffee, chatted with customers, and even managed a few lattes and cappuccinos. He knew his drinks weren't as quick or pretty as the drinks Myra made, but the customers were easy on him. Eleanor even said she appreciated his effort when Skyler delivered a maple-blackberry latte with a towering heap of whipped cream. She said it with a smile, and he didn't take offense. Her comment made him grin.

Around eight o'clock, Becca joined him, and Skyler was thankful for her expertise. She had the shop back in shape within a half hour.

Once there was a lull, Skyler took off his apron and turned to Becca. "I'll be right back. Going to check on Myra. See if she needs anything."

Becca was near the register, pouring coffee into a couple of mugs. "Take your time, bossman. I got this handled." She gave him a wink and set the carafe down. "I'll be here till closing. You do what you need to."

"Thanks, Becca," he said, and she went to deliver the fresh mugs to the back-corner booth. Myra hadn't been kidding when she'd vouched for Becca right after Skyler had first bought the shop. Becca was hardworking, outgoing, and dependable. A great employee. She and Myra were a lot alike.

Skyler hung his apron on a hook in the back hall and entered the office. He grabbed the two guitars he'd brought from home, each by the neck, and padded up the stairs to Myra's apartment. Once he was at the small landing, he set the guitars down, balancing them against the wall. He knocked softly on the door, not wanting to wake the kids if they were sleeping. The door opened slowly, revealing a surprised-looking Myra. Her dark hair was piled on the top of her head, spiraled in a messy bun that had somehow slid to the side. She was sporting baggy sweatpants topped off by a T-shirt that read *Boss Mare*. Her shirt had something smeared across the shoulder. She looked tired. And adorable. He waved.

"Hey," she said, still not opening the door all the way. "Everything okay?"

"With the shop? Yeah. All is good. I made it through the morning, and Becca saved me about an hour ago."

Myra looked relieved. "Good."

Last night, after driving Myra and the kids home, Skyler had told Myra not to worry about the shop, that he'd have it covered until the kids were feeling better. She'd looked at him like she wasn't sure what to do with the time off, but it wasn't like she was taking a vacation. She was caring for her children.

"The kids are sleeping," Myra started. "I'd invite you in, but I don't want you getting sick too. It's been a puke-cough-and-sneeze-fest in here. Germs everywhere."

He cringed, but it was mostly sympathetic. "Can I get you anything? I could run to the store."

"That's very sweet, but I think we're fine. And Mom's got dinner handled." Her eyes wandered to the two guitars on the landing behind him.

He turned so she could see them better. "I hope I'm not overstepping, but I brought a couple of guitars for the kids." They were two of his favorites: Gibson acoustics made of solid spruce. "I figured they could mess around with them when they're feeling up to it. And when they're feeling better, I could give them another lesson. If that's okay with you."

"Oh, gosh," Myra breathed. "Really? They are going to flip."

"And flipping is good?"

"Very good." Myra's excitement forced his heart to pound.

They shared a smile, and he grabbed hold of the guitars. "Where can I put them?"

Myra's excited face grew serious. "Honestly, I really don't want you to get sick."

"I'll set them inside and be on my way. Besides, I was breathing the same air as the kids in the car last night. If I was going to get sick, I'd probably be showing symptoms already."

She quirked her lips in protest but opened the door. Skyler stepped inside and could see that Myra had been cleaning. Spray bottles and a few rags littered the kitchen countertop. A mop and bucket sat near the square kitchen table. There was a basket of laundry on the couch. Half the clothes were folded, and a talk show played on the television.

"Maybe put them on the couch?" Myra asked. "Then the kids will see them right away when they wake up and come into the living room."

"Perfect." Skyler strolled over and set the guitars on the couch, opposite the laundry. He walked back to Myra.

"Thank you so much," she said, her face flushed.

"Let me know if you need anything. I'll be around." And before she could stop him, Skyler leaned in and kissed her on the cheek.

Her mouth popped open. Skyler expected to be reprimanded, but her lips slid into a smile. "You're a risky one, Mr. Clark. I sure hope you don't get sick."

He liked how she'd called him Mr. Clark. "You're worth it," he said with a grin before heading out the door.

Twelve hours later, Skyler came down with the flu.

Chapter Seventeen

"Grandma is having friends over for bridge tonight, but she's home if you guys need anything while I'm gone," Myra said to the kids as she dipped a ladle into the pot on the stove. The ladle came up full of chicken and wild rice soup, and Myra caught a whiff of onions and thyme. "But I don't want you guys going anywhere except Grandma's. It's early to bed again and back to school tomorrow." She gave Paisley and Finch a glance over her shoulder, making sure they were listening.

"I can't even go fishing with Sam?" Finch asked like he was being tortured. He was lying on his back on the living room floor, his arms and legs splayed out around him like a starfish.

"Not tonight, baby." Myra scooped along the bottom of the pot, making sure to get all the vittles at the bottom. "One more night of taking it easy. You were pretty sick, you know."

Finch propped himself up with his elbows. "But I'm not anymore."

"Finch." Myra gave him her mom-eyes. "It's almost seven o'clock. Not tonight. Finish up your puzzle or that LEGO ship you've been working on, okay? I won't be gone long."

He sighed before sitting up and scooting over to the coffee table—which was covered in LEGO and puzzle pieces. "Okay."

Myra ladled a few big scoops of soup into a container and snapped the top on. She walked over to the couch, where Paisley was snuggled in a fuzzy blanket and engrossed in some reality TV cooking competition that had a lot more yelling than cooking.

"You're in charge while I'm gone, but no fighting. Okay?" Myra said to Paisley, and she kissed her daughter on the cheek.

"Okay, Mom," Paisley agreed, her eyes glued to the TV. "Tell Skyler I hope he feels better soon. And thank you for the guitar. And I'm looking forward to more lessons." She peeled her gaze from the TV and looked at Myra.

"I will." Myra smiled.

"Is he puking like I did? Or just tired like Paisley was?" Finch asked curiously.

"Just because I didn't puke doesn't mean I wasn't sick," Paisley answered her brother, going from sweet to sassy in one second flat.

Myra rolled her eyes. She'd heard this conversation one too many times over the past two days. Finch wanted the award for being the sickest, and Paisley didn't want to talk about whatever was making her mopey. She had a case of the teenage woes. Not the flu. Myra had figured that out quickly and had pressed her daughter for what was bothering her, but Paisley had said "Nothing." Myra knew "nothing" meant "something," but also knew Paisley would open up in her own time. There was probably a friend problem or boy problem brewing, since Paisley was avoiding school. Myra would get to the bottom of it eventually.

Myra reached over and mussed Finch's hair. "You two be nice to each other while I run over to Skyler's, okay?"

"Okay," both kids responded in unison.

"Tell Skyler I've been practicing with my guitar." Finch's eyes widened in anticipation. The kids had been strumming away on their new toys since they'd gotten them. Together, they'd looked up instructional videos online, but were more excited to learn from Skyler.

"I'll tell him." Myra grabbed the still-warm container off the kitchen counter. "Love you two."

On the drive over to Skyler's house, Myra considered what she'd say to him. First, she wanted to check on him, make sure he was okay. He'd sounded horrible on the phone yesterday when he'd called to tell her he was sick. And she felt bad that he'd been a casualty of kid germs. Second, she wanted to talk to him about Perkup.

Myra had finally talked to Cedric and said she wasn't comfortable forcing Skyler into situations solely for photo ops. It bothered her that she'd agreed to Cedric's plan, not Skyler's. Cedric claimed he knew what was best for Skyler, but Myra wasn't so sure. She'd told Cedric she'd only continue to play along if Skyler was on board with the plan as well. And she couldn't accept payment in the form of Perkup. The words had been painful to say, but she couldn't accept the offer, not in good conscience. She'd worked hard for everything in her life, and she'd work just as hard to get Perkup back.

By the end of the conversation, Cedric had agreed and said he'd talk to Skyler right away. Which was good. She'd leave the music-business conversation to Cedric but wanted to address the coffee shop herself—with a proposal to buy the shop back over time.

When Myra got to Skyler's house, Carol let her in and showed her around the kitchen, getting Myra situated with a bowl, spoon, and napkins. Dorthea chatted as Myra warmed the soup in the microwave, telling Myra about the hummingbirds that loved to visit the flowers in her garden. Myra didn't think there was a garden at Skyler's place but enjoyed listening to Dorthea's story anyway. Then she followed Carol's directions and headed upstairs, stopping at the first door on the right, which was slightly ajar.

"Knock, knock," she said while rapping her knuckles against the door. "It's Myra. You decent?"

"Decent as I can be," Skyler replied, his voice raspy. "Come in."

Myra pushed the door open, exposing a big, bright bedroom that perfectly matched the exterior of the log cabin. A vaulted ceiling with exposed rustic beams oversaw a king-size bed with mussed sheets and blankets. Sun poured in from a sliding glass door and windows—all of which looked out onto a second-story deck. Skyler was on the opposite side of the room, sitting in one of two leather chairs angled toward a stone fireplace. A flat-screen television hung above the mantel. A baseball game was playing.

"Hey," Skyler greeted her. His hair looked as mussed as his bed. Dark circles lingered under his eyes. He still managed a smile.

"I brought you some sustenance." She walked over, the bowl of soup in one hand, a cold liter of ginger ale in the other.

"Thank you." He went to stand up.

"Sit. I got this." Myra placed the bowl and ginger ale on the coffee table in front of Skyler. "Carol said you had glasses up here?"

"Yeah, in the bar. To the left of the ice machine." He gestured toward the back wall, which held a high-top bar and mini fridge. *Fancy.*

"Looks like you're well stocked." There were baskets of snacks and plenty of fixings for coffee or cocktails. If she had this in her bedroom, Myra was certain she'd be carrying around an extra fifty pounds. "You don't even have to go down to the kitchen." She opened the far cabinet and found a glass.

"Good thing, because I haven't gone downstairs since I got sick. Didn't want to chance giving the flu to Grandma or Carol. Grandma just got over that nasty cough."

"Wise choice." She walked back to Skyler and set the glass on the coffee table.

"I should've listened to you and stayed out of your apartment while the kids were sick."

She nodded and filled the glass with ginger ale. "Yes, you should've." Regardless, Myra thought his gesture with the guitars was one of the sweetest things a man had ever done for her.

"Still, it was worth it." He smiled, and Myra's heart fluttered. "How are the kids doing?"

"Better. They're going back to school tomorrow. Was a twenty-four-hour bug, so hopefully you'll feel better tomorrow." She handed him the glass, and he took a sip.

"How did *you* manage not to get sick?" He was eying her like she was Superwoman.

"I've been a mom for fifteen years." Myra took a seat in the leather chair opposite Skyler. "My immune system is like Fort Knox: pretty hard to infiltrate at this point. I think my kids have exposed me to every germ on the planet."

Skyler weakly chuckled. Then he exchanged the ginger ale for the steaming bowl of soup. "You *are* like Fort Knox," he said.

She let that sink in, wondering if it was the cold medicine talking. "How so?"

"You're strong. And you've built a pretty secure wall around yourself."

"A wall?" Myra raised a brow. She was sitting in Skyler's bedroom. She'd brought him homemade soup and kissed him on a water tower. *Her* water tower. Her walls hadn't been this low in a long time.

"What I mean is, I'd like to get to know you better." His dark-circled eyes were soft; he didn't mean any harm. "I feel like I spilled my guts on the water tower and you've only just started to share glimpses of yourself with me."

Myra squinted at him, trying to decipher his comment. Did he want to get to know her as a friend? Something more? His kiss had felt like something more, but a relationship with Skyler would be complicated. "Had a lot of time to think in the past few days?"

He tilted his head. "There's only so much baseball a man can watch." He glanced at the television before scooping up a big spoonful of soup and slurping it into his mouth. His eyes closed, and he groaned. "Wow. You made this?"

Myra nodded. "Chicken and wild rice soup. It's the kids' favorite when they're sick."

He slurped another spoonful, and it put Myra at ease to see him eat. Pulling her legs up onto the chair, she tucked her socked feet under her rump and considered the walls she'd built around her heart. They were there for a reason. Each brick had been hard-earned. But there was a growing sense of comfort with Skyler. Like he was quietly removing brick after brick, giving her a view of the other side.

"What do you want to know?" she asked quietly.

Licking soup off his lower lip, Skyler let the spoon sink back into the bowl. "Have you always lived in Maple Bay?"

"Mostly." She paused after her one-word answer.

"Are you going to make me guess where else you've lived?" He pressed her with a stare. "Miami? London? Tokyo?"

She cracked a grin, almost wanting to let him keep guessing. "Are those all places you've been?"

"Yes, but you're not answering *my* question."

She rested her hand on her thigh and picked at the seam of her jeans. "I was born here, grew up here, and don't plan to leave. But I traveled a lot in my early twenties. I practically lived out of a horse trailer. Hauled my horse all across the country, going to rodeos."

"By yourself?"

"Sometimes." She shrugged. "But most of the time, I was hauling with at least one of my cousins. Besides, you're never really alone at a rodeo. You get to know the other competitors. It becomes like a family on the road."

"Sounds a lot like being a musician." He said it like the similarities were overwhelming. Maybe they were. Except Skyler was singing to sold-out stadiums, raking in millions. Myra loved rodeo with all her heart, but she'd barely made enough money on the winnings to continue competing, let alone to support herself.

"Do you miss your band?" she asked, wondering if he considered them family.

"I miss the guys and the music. I don't miss being on the road." He ate another spoonful of soup before setting the bowl on the coffee table. "Why'd you stop?"

"Traveling the country?"

He nodded.

"I met Luis and had Paisley." She'd been twenty-two when she met Luis—at a rodeo in Nevada—and had given birth to Paisley not long after her twenty-third birthday.

"You moved back here to have a family?"

"I moved back here to be with my family."

His eyebrow dipped like he wasn't following.

Thinking back to when Paisley was a baby, Myra remembered how she'd struggled with the decision to pause her rodeo career.

She'd wanted to do a million things before she settled down and had a family, but she'd let herself get wrapped up in a man, and her plans had changed. "I met Luis on the rodeo circuit. He rode bulls. I ran barrels. We had a whirlwind romance. I got pregnant." She ran her teeth over her bottom lip, remembering the stares, the judgment.

Skyler made a noise of agreement with his throat. "And you came back home when you were pregnant with Paisley?"

"It was the best thing for Paisley. And for me." Myra's gaze fell to the bowl of soup on the coffee table. The soup was Judy's recipe. Her mom used to make it for Myra when she was young. And when she was pregnant. "Neither of my parents were happy when I first told them I was pregnant, and they were really upset when Luis and I had the brilliant idea to elope. But they were there for me when I needed them. Even though they didn't agree with my decisions. And I really don't know what I would've done without my mom. She was my rock. Having a baby was terrifying."

Skyler grinned at her. "But you figured it out."

"Mostly," she replied. "I mean, sometimes I still wonder if I know what I'm doing."

"As a mom?"

Myra shrugged one shoulder. "Parenting is hard. I constantly question myself and wonder if I'm doing or saying the right thing. Honestly, I didn't understand the heartache I gave my parents when I got pregnant and eloped. Not until after I became a mother. Now I know they only wanted the best for me. They saw all the red flags long before I did."

"With Luis?"

Myra nodded. "They were trying their best to steer me in the safest direction, and I didn't want to listen. Luis continued to rodeo, and we fumbled through another ten years of marriage. We are better off divorced, but Paisley and Finch are the best things that ever happened to me. They're my heart."

Skyler gazed at her, thoughtfully. "I can tell. They're lucky to have a mom like you."

She was lucky to have them. "You never wanted to have kids?"

Skyler ran his thumb back and forth over the leather armrest. "It was never the right time or the right person. Music always came first, but if I'm being honest, I always wondered what it would be like. To be a dad."

"You'd be good at it," Myra said, thinking about how sweet he was with her kids. "You'd figure it out. Just like everyone else."

For a fleeting moment, Myra pictured Skyler as a stepfather. Then panic seized her chest. She couldn't make that mistake twice. She wasn't about to fall for someone that would leave her in the dust. After re-signing with his label, Skyler would go back on the road, and Myra couldn't let her heart—or her kids—get used to him in any capacity other than as a friend or boss. Eventually, he'd leave.

"Why'd you choose Maple Bay?" She spoke the words almost as they hit her brain.

Skyler ran a hand over his jaw, which was starting to sport a dark five o'clock shadow. "I needed to get away."

Myra knew Cedric had advised Skyler to do so. "But you could've gone anywhere. How did you pick Maple Bay, Minnesota?" She'd wondered this since he stepped foot in her coffee shop.

"Actually, there's something I'd like to show you." Skyler stood and walked to his dresser. When he came back, he raised something in his hand. "Remember when I asked you about that old photo of the barn? The one I found in your files?" Skyler sat on the edge of the coffee table, directly in front of Myra. He handed her a black-and-white photograph. Myra studied it.

"Yes, but this is a different photo." Like the others, the picture showed the barn long before it had become Perkup. But it also showed a beautiful woman smiling and posing for the camera. Myra cocked her head, still staring at the snapshot. "Did you find this in my files as well?" She'd never seen this one before.

When she looked up, Skyler shook his head. "That's my grand-ma."

Myra's gaze fell back to the image. She blinked, not sure what was going on. "This is Dorthea?"

"Yes." He took hold of the photo and turned it around. On the back, there was writing: *Maple Bay, Minnesota, 1956.*

Myra stared at the ink like she'd fallen into the Twilight Zone.

Skyler turned the photograph back around. "Photos trigger memories for my grandma, and she always lights up when she sees this one." He pointed to the picture. "She told me about a wedding she attended in this barn. She couldn't remember names but went on and on about the band and the dance."

Myra looked at Skyler, astounded. "Did you move here because of this picture?"

"It sounds crazy when you say it out loud," he replied. "But yes."

Myra scanned Skyler's face—the way his eyes watched her, like he was waiting for her reaction. Or maybe her approval. "You moved here for your grandma," she whispered. It wasn't a question. She knew how important Dorthea was to Skyler.

He nodded. "I bought Perkup for her too." He gripped the edge of the coffee table, his hands pressed next to his thighs. "I thought if I surrounded my grandma with enough memories, I could keep her from forgetting."

Myra's mouth opened and closed. A lump filled her throat. Skyler's explanation took her breath away. He'd lost a lot in the past year—a marriage, a career. And now he was losing his grandma.

She shifted forward, to the edge of the chair, and reached for him. Skyler took her hand in his and set their intertwined fingers on his leg.

This wasn't the right time to talk about what she needed. The shop wasn't going anywhere. She'd talk to Skyler about buying it back another day.

"What are you thinking?" Skyler asked, staring at her with the eyes of a man who knew how to love.

"I think we should take Dorthea on an outing. To Perkup."

Chapter Eighteen

The Maple Bay fairgrounds didn't look like much, but Skyler could tell the dirt arena, metal bleachers, and surrounding barns held a special place in Myra's heart. She hadn't stopped smiling since he arrived. Secretly, Skyler wished her smile was solely the result of his presence. But he knew better. Currently, she was riding across the arena on her horse, Charm. Her kids, mom, and extended family were either perched on horses or hanging out in the bleachers. A good chunk of the town's population had joined them.

"Perfect weather for a rodeo practice," Judy said, ambling over to join Skyler. He stood at the fence, watching the commotion in the arena. Mostly, he was watching Myra, marveling at her riding skills and bright smile. As Myra rode Charm across the arena, her raven hair rolled and bounced over her back. She sported a black cowboy hat and was the best-looking cowgirl he'd ever seen. And he'd seen plenty.

He smiled at Judy. "It's a beautiful night." A chill had hit the air since Skyler had arrived an hour ago, but it was still warm enough for him to be comfortable in a flannel. The arena lights turned on, buzzing above their heads, as the evening sky melted into pinks and lavenders. "Myra said the local rodeo committee hosts practices here once a week?"

"When the weather allows." Judy set her hands on her hips. "Ain't nobody riding horses out here in January when it's below zero." She laughed.

"I bet," Skyler replied, knowing neither Los Angeles nor Nashville had given him much experience with snow or subzero temps. "How cold does it get here in the winter?"

"Oh, *plenty* cold." She belly laughed and gave him a pat on the arm. "You'll see. I hope you've got a warm coat."

Skyler was a little shocked by how easily Judy had mentioned him staying for the winter—which was half a year away. However, he also liked the idea of staying put. Of not going back on the road. He was enjoying the simple luxuries of life. *Friends. Family. Community.*

Spending time with a certain raven-haired cowgirl who had mesmerized his heart.

Across the arena, a cow burst out of a chute. Two horses and riders galloped after it. The metal clang and thunder of hooves grabbed both Skyler and Judy's attention.

"Get 'em, Creed!" Judy yelled as one rider looped a rope in circles above his cowboy hat. He released the rope, tossing it at the running cow. The lasso slid over the animal's horned head.

Instantly, the second rider threw his rope at the cow's back legs, putting a lasso in the perfect spot to sneak under the cow's running hooves. Skyler didn't understand how that was even possible.

"Yeehaw, Evan!" Judy threw a fist in the air as both men eased their horses to a stop, keeping their ropes tight and stilling the roped cow. "Oh, those boys are a good team!"

"Sure looks like it," Skyler agreed.

As the cow was released, Myra and her cousin Kat rode in, directing the animal back to the pen. Again, Skyler watched Myra, entranced by how natural she looked in the saddle. After the cow was penned, Myra waved at him from across the arena. He waved back. So did Judy.

Judy chuckled, breaking Skyler out of his Myra-trance.

"See something interesting?" Judy winked like she'd just caught Skyler with his hand in the cookie jar. She had.

He stood up straight. "Uh, yeah. This roping stuff is pretty interesting." Skyler wiped his face clean of what had actually been running through his mind. Kissing Myra on the water tower. Watching the baseball game with her while sipping homemade soup. How she swept into every situation and took control. How sweet she was when she let him in.

"You should try it sometime," Judy suggested.

"Roping?" He assumed Judy was *not* referring to her daughter.

"Sure. Why not? I'm sure we could wrangle a horse for you to ride."

Skyler smirked. "Maybe someday." Then he cleared his throat, mostly to clear his head. If he was *considering* climbing into a saddle, he was in deep.

Looking past Judy, to the bleachers, Skyler tried to take his mind off the feelings that were invading his heart. He had a whole list of reasons to ignore those impulses, but the ink on that list was starting to fade. "I should check on Grandma," Skyler said.

"Oh, child. Dorthea is fine. Do you see that smile on her face?" Judy turned, and they both caught Dorthea giggling. She sat on the bottom row of the bleachers. Carol was perched on one side of her, and Myra's aunt Joyce lounged on the other. All three ladies were fawning over a little blonde girl—Myra's niece, Charlie. She wore jeans, pink cowboy boots, and pigtails, and she was doing some type of tap dance. Everyone seemed fully entertained.

"You need to bring Dorthea around more often. She's a doll," Judy said. "Bring her to Sunday service and then family supper at Joyce and Gene's. We'd love to have you over. Carol too."

Skyler's heart squeezed like someone had lassoed it and pulled the rope tight. "Thanks, Judy. I'd really like that. And I know Grandma and Carol would too."

"It's settled, then. You all come over this Sunday, okay?" Judy winked but didn't wait for Skyler's reply. Instead, she headed back toward the bleachers. She clapped for Charlie as she approached. Dorthea joined in on the applause, and Charlie ate up the attention. Her little blonde pigtails bounced like crazy as she tapped away, her hands on her hips.

"She's a ham, isn't she?" Myra asked from the arena. She was on foot, walking toward Skyler. Behind her, Paisley rode away on Charm.

"Sure is," Skyler replied.

Myra climbed over the fence, and Skyler helped her down. When she landed in front of him, he forced his hands to stay where they were. He wanted to grab her and plant a kiss on top of her smile.

Instead of giving in to his urge, he asked, "Paisley going to chase cows for a bit?"

"Steers, you mean?" Myra laughed and hooked a thumb toward the arena. "There's not one *cow* in there."

Skyler squinted at her. "Cows. Steers. Sounds like a technicality to me."

"I think most cowboys would beg to differ."

"You mean steer-boys?" he challenged her.

She pressed a hand to her chest with another laugh. "You have a point, but you might want to keep that to yourself. We take our cattle and horses pretty seriously around here."

Nothing about Myra felt serious at that moment. Was she flirting with him? Out in the open for everyone to see? The thought gave his chest a zing.

"Mom, you want a pop?" Finch yelled as he ran toward the turquoise trailer that Myra and Skyler had hauled over earlier.

The trailer was an old two-horse trailer that Myra had converted into a mobile coffee shop. The inside had been gutted and filled with cabinets, a sink, an espresso machine, and coffee makers. A window on the side pulled down and served as a pass-through. She stored the trailer at her aunt and uncle's property and took it to rodeos to make extra cash.

Earlier today, Myra had told Skyler that she'd been bringing the trailer to rodeo practice for the last few years and always donated refreshments. He'd loved that and wanted to help, so he and Myra had gone grocery shopping. They'd filled the trailer with pop, waters, and snacks. He'd had to fight her to pay for the grocery bill.

"You thirsty?" Myra asked Skyler. He nodded, and they walked toward the trailer. "Grab me a Coke, Finchy."

"You want something, Sky?" Finch asked as he handed his mom a cold pop from the cooler next to the trailer. Skyler loved how Finch had called him *Sky* right from the start.

"I'll take a Coke too, Finchy. Thanks."

Finch handed Skyler an icy can. Then he ran off, saying something about running the chutes with his uncle Evan.

Myra took a swig of her drink. The brim of her black cowboy hat tipped up to the pink sky.

Skyler opened his pop. It hissed. "I think I'll bring Grandma by the shop tomorrow after closing. If she's up for it. I'd love it if you and the kids could be there." Today had gone well, giving Skyler high hopes for tomorrow. "Maybe the shop will bring back memories. Maybe it won't. But I know she loves spending time with you and the kids."

Myra cocked her head like he'd asked her a crazy question. "Of course we'll be there. Wouldn't miss it. What time? And what kind of cookies does she like? I'd like to make her a treat."

Skyler grinned at Myra's sweetness. "Three o'clock? And I've never seen my grandma turn down a cookie. She loves them all."

"My kind of woman," Myra replied just as a timer beeped from inside the trailer, indicating the automatic shutoff for the coffee maker. "I should make one more pot of coffee."

"I'll help." Skyler followed Myra into the trailer through the open back doors. Once inside, she went to the cabinets at the front and retrieved a bag of grounds. Skyler grabbed the coffee pot and filled it with water at the sink. As he did, Myra situated a fresh filter and grounds into the coffee maker.

"Don't want to short anyone on their caffeine consumption," Myra jested.

"Certainly not," Skyler replied. Once the pot was full of water, he joined Myra at the coffee maker. His eyes met hers, and it was immediately apparent how close they were in the small space of the trailer. When she unabashedly returned his gaze, his pulse picked up.

Skyler set the pot on the counter before he spilled it. "What would you say if I told you I wanted to kiss you?"

"I'd say you better get to it," she replied without missing a beat. Then she stepped back from the pass-through window to an area of the trailer that was more private. Skyler followed.

He reached for her hand and weaved his fingers into hers before sliding their intertwined hands against Myra's lower back. "The hat might have to go," he whispered, gently pulling her close.

She grinned up at him. "It comes off."

With his free hand, Skyler tipped Myra's cowboy hat to the back of her head, pushing the brim up and exposing her beautiful face. He leaned in and brushed his lips to hers, wondering if he could make this a regular occurrence. As they kissed, Skyler lost himself in the moment. His lips tried to tell Myra how his feelings for her had grown. They'd snuck up on him like a heart attack.

"Mom?" Paisley called from somewhere outside the trailer. "Can you come take Charm?" There was an urgency in Paisley's voice, and Myra pulled back.

"Hold that thought." Myra released Skyler's hand and exited the trailer.

Skyler took a second to gather his composure. Then he turned back to the coffee maker, intending to finish prepping the pot. However, the pieces of conversation he caught between Myra and Paisley made him stop. Was Paisley crying?

Skyler stepped out of the trailer to see what was happening.

Myra had climbed over the fence and was in the arena. Paisley was off Charm, standing on the ground and holding the horse by the reins. She didn't look injured, but as Skyler neared, he saw tears streaming down her face. He also noticed Paisley's dad walking across the arena. As Luis got close, Paisley shoved Charm's reins at her mother. Myra took hold, and her daughter ran off.

Skyler jumped on the fence and leapt over, wanting to get to Myra. "She okay?"

Myra turned to face him. Her usual boldness had drained from her face. "Can you hold Charm?"

"Yeah." He took the reins from Myra. "What else can I do?"

"I've got to talk to Paisley. Just stay here. Take care of Charm, please." She touched his arm before jogging off after her daughter.

Skyler watched helplessly as Myra retreated. Luis trailed her.

Skyler wanted to step in, to soothe whatever had upset Paisley and Myra. Instead, he watched as they ran off toward one of the barns. Then he noticed a woman following the crew. She ran up behind Luis and took his hand. It was the same woman Skyler had seen at Luis' house the night he and Myra had picked up the kids.

Skyler's stomach sank. What new trouble had dropped on Myra and the kids he was coming to adore?

Chapter Nineteen

"Paisley?" Myra called as she jogged into the barn and down the concrete aisle. Stopping, she listened for her daughter, but the barn was empty and quiet. It was only used during rodeos and shows when horses stayed overnight. For practice, everyone hauled their horses in and kept them at their trailers when they weren't riding. "Where you at, honey?"

No response.

Myra peeked in empty stalls. She stepped into the show office and poked around.

No sign of her daughter. She called out for her again before remembering an incident from last year at Maple Bay Days. Paisley had run barrels on Charm for the first time at a big event and her nerves had gotten the best of her. During her run, she'd panicked, knocked over two barrels, and Charm had even bucked. She'd been so upset and had ended up sitting on the grassy knoll behind the farthest barn, licking her wounds for a few hours. Thinking Paisley might have gone to the same place, Myra headed toward the far barn. She gave a sigh of relief when she rounded the back side of the building and discovered her daughter.

Paisley was sitting in the grass, her back against the barn and her arms wrapped around her knees. She acknowledged Myra with a glance before looking out over freshly planted corn fields. Myra walked over and took a seat next to her daughter. They sat there in silence, watching as a few pickups and a semi buzzed down the road in the distance.

"Can you tell me what happened?" Myra asked, only knowing the few pieces of information Paisley had given her in the arena. She didn't want to ride any more tonight. And something Luis said had upset her.

Paisley looked down at her knees. As Myra patiently waited for her daughter to talk, she gingerly tucked Paisley's hair behind her ear.

"I asked Dad about something I heard at school." Paisley sniffled, still looking down.

Myra's chest stilled; she wasn't sure what Paisley could've heard at school. "Is that the reason you were upset earlier this week? Why you wanted to stay home from school even though you weren't sick?"

"Yeah," Paisley admitted. Then she took a breath and looked at Myra. Pain was apparent behind her sweet eyes. "Jeanie Cooper told me that Dad's girlfriend is pregnant."

"Kathy is pregnant?" Myra's chest clenched, and she tried her best not to let the shock show on her face. Luis and Kathy had only been dating for a few months. *At most.* Luis had just recently introduced her to the kids as his girlfriend.

Myra swallowed and closed her gaping mouth. "And how would Jeanie know that?"

"She said she overheard her mom and Kathy talking about it. I didn't want to say anything until I knew for sure, but I asked Dad tonight. He said it's true." Paisley's voice wavered.

Myra took Paisley's hand, peeling it away from her knees. "Baby, I wish you'd told me what was going on," Myra said. Her daughter had been grappling with this information all week. By herself. "You can tell me anything. Anytime. I'm serious. If you're hurting, I want to know so I can help. I'm here for you, no matter what."

Paisley nodded, slowly. A tear slipped over her cheek. "I didn't want it to be true. I thought maybe Jeanie heard wrong, or she was lying."

"Oh, sweetie," Myra cooed as she considered killing Luis for letting Paisley find out this way.

"Why would Dad do that?" Paisley's question came out in a squeak.

Get his girlfriend pregnant? Keep a secret from his kids? Myra scrambled to think of an appropriate response. How long had he known Kathy was pregnant? When had he planned to tell the kids? Or tell her? He was a grown man and should know better—on all kinds of levels.

Instead of directly addressing Paisley's question, Myra wrapped an arm around Paisley's shoulders and pulled her into a hug. Paisley rested her head against Myra's chest. "I'm sorry you found out this way," Myra said as she rubbed her daughter's back. "I don't think your dad intended for that to happen. Can you tell me what you're most upset about? Other than how you found out."

"I just . . ." Paisley paused, sounding like her next words had gotten stuck in her throat. "It's just that Dad has been spending all his time with Kathy. They go to rodeos together. She's always at the house when he's home. I never get to spend any time with him by myself anymore. And now he's going to have a baby with her. Finch and I are never going to see him."

Myra's stomach rolled. She wanted to jump up, run to Luis, and scream at him for hurting Paisley. Instead, she said, "Your dad loves you, Paisley. That will never change. A new relationship doesn't change that. A new baby doesn't change that. But you need to tell your dad how you're feeling. You need to tell him what you just told me. He needs to hear that. I know he doesn't want to hurt you."

Myra yearned to take away her daughter's pain. She wanted to squelch every fear. It tore her insides apart to know she couldn't fix this for her kids. The best she could do was guide them through the path ahead. It was going to be a rocky road, but she'd hold them through every bump.

Paisley sniffled and nodded against Myra's chest. "Will you talk to Dad with me?"

"Of course." Myra kissed Paisley on the top of her head. Then they went to find Luis.

After a painful talk, during which Myra had to bite her tongue multiple times, she walked back to the arena with Paisley, feeling a little numb. Rodeo practice was wrapping up. Riders were dismounting. Horses were being loaded into trailers.

"I'm going to go sit in the truck, okay?" Paisley's eyes were red from tears.

"Sure, baby. I'll close up the trailer and get Finch. Then we'll go home."

As Paisley climbed into the truck, Myra entered the attached coffee trailer and started cleaning up. As she closed the pass-through window, Skyler stepped in through the back.

"Hey," he said, his eyes creased at the corners in concern. "Everything okay?"

She paused, wanting to tell him what happened but also knowing Luis had yet to sit down with Finch to break the news. She didn't think Skyler would tell a soul, but at this point, she wasn't willing to chance it. Plus, if she was being honest with herself, she was having a hard time swallowing the news herself. Myra hadn't expected the unsettling déjà vu that had crept over her as she'd listened to Luis explain himself to Paisley. As he'd talked, Myra's mind had flitted back to when she was first pregnant. All she'd wanted was a sense of stability from Luis, but he had been more interested in riding bulls than taking care of her. It was then that she'd learned being with a man did not guarantee security. She could only provide that for herself.

Skyler put his hand on her arm, jerking her from her thoughts. "Myra?"

She looked up at him. "Paisley's okay. She's upset about something that happened at school." It was a fraction of the truth.

"Oh." Skyler didn't look convinced, but Myra wasn't ready to rehash what had just happened.

"Thanks for taking Charm," she added, realizing Skyler had grabbed hold of the reins even though he was leery of horses. He hadn't even hesitated.

"No problem." Skyler put a hand in his jeans pocket. "Kat took him. Said she'd get him home."

Myra nodded and absentmindedly tucked a few odds and ends back in the cabinets. At least she didn't have to worry about Charm. She knew Kat would take care of her horse.

"Okay. Well, I'm going to get Grandma and Carol back to the house. Unless you need any help?" His question was tentative, like he was waiting for her to spill what was really going on.

"No, that's okay. I'm going to round up Finch and get going. I'll just park the trailer behind Perkup for the night."

Luis had said he'd stop by and talk with Finch tonight. She had another intense conversation ahead of her and no room in her brain for anything else. Did she want to lean on Skyler? Yes, but the thought frightened her. It had been a long time since she'd let herself lean on a man. And in her experience, life was steadier when she stood on her own two feet.

"All right." Skyler took a step back. "Call me if you need anything."

She forced a smile, mostly to cover the worry and doubt rolling through her head. She couldn't handle any more questions. Not tonight. "Good night," she said.

"Good night, Myra." Skyler left the trailer.

Myra leaned against the counter and took a deep breath. She wanted to stop Skyler, to let him wrap her in a hug, but this moment wasn't about her. It was about her kids. So she closed the trailer, found Finch, and drove her kids home.

Chapter Twenty

Later that night, Skyler sat on his deck, sipping a glass of bourbon and fighting his instinct to reach out to Myra. She'd seemed upset when he'd left, but he didn't think pushing the topic would be wise. Not with Myra. She was very protective of her kids—rightfully so—but Skyler still wanted her to know he was there for her if she needed him. Even if it was just to bend his ear. Deciding to send her a quick message, Skyler set his drink down and picked up his phone. Cedric's texts glared up at him from the screen.

Cedric: *You up? Can you talk?*

His following texts contained links. Skyler clicked through them to discover articles mentioning his name on all the major entertainment outlets. The headlines read like a political campaign for a small-town mayor. *Skyler Ridge Finds His Country Roots. Ridge Gives Up Penthouse for Small Town. Country Roads Lead Skyler Ridge Home.*

He scanned the photos. Most were from tonight—taken just a few hours ago.

Skyler groaned and felt his blood pressure rise. There were photos of him leaning against the fence, watching the roping. Other pictures showed him sipping coffee while smiling and talking with Myra's family. And there were plenty that showed him standing in the arena holding Charm.

Even here, in Maple Bay, there was no way to get away from the media. Would he ever have privacy? A life that wasn't broadcast for the world to see?

Skyler ran a hand over his face, not sure what to do. Were the stories bad? Not this time. That didn't mean the media wouldn't twist their next ones in a different light. Any time he went out in public with Myra, her kids, or her other family members, he was throwing them in front of the hungry, judgmental paparazzi. Who knew what the media would say next?

And who was taking these photos? Someone was obviously keeping tabs on him or getting tips from someone in Maple Bay.

Another message appeared from Cedric.

Cedric: *Call me. I've got good news!*

Skyler started to reply but promptly deleted his message, not wanting to talk with Cedric tonight. However, his quick fingers had alerted Cedric of his presence.

The phone rang.

"Crap," Skyler said to the empty porch. He took a swig of bourbon and answered the call. "Hey."

"Hey, hey," Cedric replied, sounding way too enthusiastic. "I didn't want to wake you, but I have some fabulous news!"

Skyler braced himself for what was to come, not sure it was going to be good. "What is it?"

"The label," Cedric huffed into the phone. "Country Records loves everything you've been doing. The horses. The rodeo. The cowgirl. All the small-town wholesomeness. It's fabulous, and fans are talking. They want to see more. And they want their superstar back."

Skyler searched for words but came up empty. Cedric made it sound like Skyler had been acting since he'd stepped foot in Maple Bay. He hadn't been. He wasn't using the town or Myra to repair his image. He was just . . . living.

"So, *now* the label is interested in me again?" Skyler asked, remembering how quickly they'd dumped him when the news stories weren't as appealing. "Because my image aligns with their brand?"

"Yes!" Cedric responded.

His enthusiasm irked Skyler, but he tried not to take his frustrations out on Cedric. This was Cedric's job: to manage Skyler's career. It was just that Skyler and Cedric weren't headed down the same road anymore. Maybe hadn't been for a long time.

"And they want you to sing at the Country Music Awards on Sunday! They said it can be your comeback performance!"

"Sunday?" It was Friday night now. And he had a dinner date on Sunday.

"They've already set up a private jet to leave from Brainerd, so you don't have to drive all the way to Minneapolis." Cedric continued with more details about lavish parties and designer clothes, but Skyler felt like he'd been pushed from his chair and thumped to the floor.

"They just expect me to pick up and jump at their beck and call?" Skyler interrupted. "Like a puppet? Did they ever think to ask me if I *wanted* to sing at the CMAs? Actually, did anyone from the label think to ask me how I was doing in the past few weeks?"

There was a very long pause on the other end of the phone. "Skyler, you already committed to singing at the CMAs." All the wind had been knocked from Cedric's sails.

"That was before Country Records pulled me and the band from the show when I failed to meet their brand standards. Now they've changed their mind? Everything's okay again?"

"I mean," Cedric said, fumbling for words, which was out of character for him. "Everyone is expecting you to be there. The label. The fans. They're going to start advertising it tonight."

"I don't know . . ." Skyler trailed off. Why should he bend to the whims of a company that didn't care about him? "I don't think I can do it."

The loud clatter of Cedric dropping his phone sounded in Skyler's ear. A few seconds later, he was back. "Look, I hate to be the bearer of bad news, but you're still under contract with them. If you don't show up for the CMAs, it'll be a breach of contract. They could sue you and your band. You know how lawyer-happy the label is."

Skyler sighed. He didn't want to put his band at risk. If it came down to it, he'd do it just for their sake. "I need to sleep on it," he said reluctantly.

"Okay," Cedric said, and he gave Skyler exactly one night to think. The next morning, Cedric showed up in Maple Bay.

Chapter Twenty-One

Myra's cell phone dinged. She was snuggled up with her kids on the couch, and she gently slid her phone from her sweatshirt pocket, trying not to move too much. She didn't want to rouse Paisley or Finch, who were both sound asleep. Paisley's legs stretched across Myra's thighs. Finch was snuggled into the crook of her arm. One of their favorite movies played on the TV, and Myra was thankful to have her babies near. She was grateful to be there for them in a confusing time, to let them know all would be okay. No matter what.

When she tapped her phone, she saw that Skyler had texted her.

Skyler: *If you need to talk to someone, I promise I'm a good listener. Call or text, no matter the hour. Hope everything is okay.*

His text warmed her heart. It gave her relief. Then she stared at her phone for a few minutes, not sure how to answer. Could she let her guard down? Trust someone who had the potential to hurt her and her kids? Conflicting emotions battled against each other until her fingers finally tapped against her phone.

Myra: *Thanks for checking in. We're okay, but I'd like to tell you what happened. Tomorrow?*

Skyler: *Sure thing. Sweet dreams.*

Myra: *Good night.*

The next morning, Myra opened the shop with Becca. The Saturday crowd trickled in about eight o'clock, so Myra had plenty of time to think as she brewed coffee and stocked bagels, croissants, and muffins in the glass case. She thought about the first time she'd met Skyler—which could've been classified as one of the worst days of her life. Her choices had compounded into one explosive moment in which everything she'd worked for had been ripped from her. At the time, she hadn't even considered that Skyler would turn into someone she would be excited to see each and every day. He continued to show her that she could trust him—maybe even lean on him—but should she open her heart to him if he wasn't going to stick around? Skyler wasn't made to live in a small town. He was meant to sing on stages across the world. Their lives couldn't align in the way her heart yearned for, so she smothered the yearning with a dose of reality.

Skyler wouldn't give up music. Even if he kept the coffee shop, eventually, he'd be back on the stage. And she couldn't build a life with someone that lived on the road. She'd tried that before.

Still, her heart wanted to.

As the bell jingled and the front door opened, Myra placed the last croissant in the glass case. She turned to greet the customer, hoping it was Skyler. Instead, she laid her eyes on Cedric. Just like the first time she met him, he looked out of place, dressed as if he were going to a wedding. Though this time, the look on his face said he might be on his way to a funeral.

He strode toward her. "Can we talk?" His tone was urgent.

Myra's chest tightened. "Uh, sure. The office?"

Cedric nodded, and Myra led him to the back of the shop, letting Becca know she'd return in a few minutes. Becca gave her a questioning look. The handful of customers in the shop watched curiously, but Myra ignored their stares. As soon as she stepped into the office, Cedric started talking.

"Look, we had a deal." He stood next to the metal folding chair, nearly pacing. Myra edged behind the desk. "All you had to do was put Skyler in a few situations where he could be photographed. I would take care of the rest. I'd fix his image."

"And I did that," she replied. Why was Cedric so riled up?

"Barely," he seethed.

Myra didn't like his tone. "Why are you here, Cedric? Did you talk to Skyler about the pictures? I told you I would help with more as long as Skyler was on board with the plan."

Cedric placed a hand on the back of the chair. "I'm here to make sure Skyler doesn't make another mistake."

Myra scrunched her brow. Cedric hadn't answered her question. "What are you talking about?"

"I think you've got Skyler under some kind of spell. What have you been telling him?" Cedric's stare narrowed like he was truly looking at a witch. "Skyler's got a big heart. He falls in love too easily. And I think you're just another gold digger coming for his money."

If Myra's eyes could've popped out of her head, they would've. "Excuse me? Did you just call me a gold digger? I am certainly *not* after Skyler's money, and I think you'd better . . ." She raised her finger, pointing to the door.

"You signed that contract pretty quickly when I handed it over to you." Cedric raised an eyebrow. "You wanted this coffee shop back, and you had no problem agreeing to dupe Skyler to make that happen."

Myra stopped breathing. Her pointing hand still hung in the air. "I didn't," she started, wanting to say that she'd never meant to hurt Skyler—but when she'd signed the contract, she hadn't been thinking about him. She'd been focused on herself. All she'd been worried about was getting her business back.

"I'm on the verge of getting Skyler a new contract with Country Records, and he doesn't even want to consider it," Cedric said. "I've seen all the pictures of the two of you together. My photographer has been following Skyler around for weeks. I've seen the photos of the two of you canoodling and kissing. What do you think Skyler would say if I showed him the contract you signed?" Cedric's voice was sharp. His gaze bored into her.

Myra swallowed, knowing exactly what Skyler would think if Cedric threw that contract in his face. Especially if Skyler had signed the contract without being fully aware of its contents.

Skyler would think Myra was using him. That her feelings for him weren't real.

"What do you want from me?" Her jaw clenched, holding back what she wanted to say to Cedric—that he was a sleaze. Clearly, Cedric didn't have Skyler's best interests in mind.

"I want you to convince Skyler that he needs to talk with Country Records. That he needs to sign another contract with them." Cedric released his grip from the back of the chair. "If he does that, I'll rip up the contract you signed, and it will never see the light of day. Then you and Skyler can continue this little tryst, and he'll never be the wiser."

The word *tryst* made Myra's gut turn. That wasn't what was happening. At least, not in her eyes. She cared about Skyler, and she was not about to lie to him. Not anymore.

"Okay," she said. "I'll talk to him."

She'd talk to him, all right. She'd tell Skyler *exactly* what he needed to know.

Chapter Twenty-Two

That morning, Cedric called, letting Skyler know he'd landed in Minnesota and was driving toward Maple Bay. He wanted to talk to Skyler face to face—make sure he understood the possible ramifications of not fulfilling his contract with the label. Skyler agreed, but only because he was considering other people who relied on him. His band understood he was on the verge of quitting the music industry. They supported him, but he also didn't want them involved in a lawsuit just because Skyler hadn't shown up for one performance. Furthermore, he owed it to Cedric to finish his contract with Country Records. Cedric had represented Skyler for the better part of a decade, and he deserved to get his slice of the pie as well. Skyler could handle one more performance and fulfill his obligations through the end of his contract. But that was it.

However, before Cedric arrived, Myra called. She asked if Skyler could meet her at Joyce and Gene's barn to talk, and Skyler immediately agreed, figuring she wanted to tell him what had happened last night with Paisley.

However, when he parked at the entrance of the barn, Myra waved at him with a timidness that was unlike her. She stood in the aisle next to Charm's stall. Charm hung his head over the stall door, and Myra scratched his chin.

Skyler got out of his car and walked into the barn. "Hey, you've got me a little worried." There was a heavy air about her. "Is everything okay?"

"No, it's not." She shook her head and offered her hand. "Can we talk?"

He nodded, and she laced her fingers through his. She led him to the middle of the barn and sat on a stack of hay bales.

"What's going on?" He sat down beside her. Was she upset about last night? About the news stories and pictures in the media?

"I need to tell you something." She looked at him, her ice-blue eyes pained. "But first, I need you to know that I care about you. I honestly do. And I never want to hurt you. Not ever again. That's why I need to tell you the truth."

He tightened his grip on her hand. "You can tell me," he urged.

Myra tucked her hair behind an ear and took a breath. "The day you bought Perkup, I was extremely hurt. I felt like my world was crumbling down on top of me, and I didn't know how I'd pick up the pieces. I'd lost my business and my home. Things I'd worked hard to build. I panicked. I felt like I'd lost everything I'd worked for, and I didn't know how I'd move on."

Skyler turned toward her. Their knees touched. "Myra, I see how hard you work. I know how passionate you are about Perkup." It was the reason he'd thought about signing the shop back to her. When they'd first met, he'd thought Myra had run the business into the ground, but now he saw firsthand how she put her whole heart and soul into Perkup—just like she did for everyone and everything she cared about. "I understand now what was going through your head that day."

She bit her bottom lip. "No matter what was happening in my life, I still shouldn't have done what I did." Skyler searched her gaze, looking for clarity, but then she added, "The day you bought the shop, Cedric came to see me."

Skyler's mind lulled to a stop. "Cedric? My agent?"

She nodded. "He made me an offer."

A chill ran over Skyler, prickling his skin. Cedric had never mentioned that he'd met Myra or been to the shop. "What kind of offer?" His question formed slowly. He wasn't sure he wanted the answer.

"He told me your image needed to be repaired, that you needed to be portrayed in a certain way in order to get your music career back." Myra shook her head back and forth. "He said that if I could make you look like a cowboy, you'd have a better chance of getting a new contract with your label. So, I agreed. I put you in a few staged situations, and Cedric had a photographer take pictures."

"Pictures? The photos of me and you?"

"Yes," she said. "And Cedric also gave me a contract. It said that if I helped facilitate the pictures, that I would get Perkup back."

Skyler blinked, not able to absorb what Myra was telling him. "A contract?" he asked. That didn't make sense. "But I would've needed to sign that. The shop is in my name."

"You signed it. I saw your signature before I added mine."

Confusion and hurt intertwined in his chest. Cedric had been Skyler's agent for years. Had he forged Skyler's signature? Or made Skyler think he was signing something else?

And what part had Myra truly played in all of this?

"I shouldn't have agreed to do it," Myra said. "In the moment, I thought it was the best thing to do. For me. And probably for you too. I'd get the shop back, and you could go back to singing. But as I got to know you, I realized how important your privacy was and that you weren't even sure about continuing with Country Records. So I told Cedric I was out, that I'd only help with the photos if that was what *you* wanted. Cedric said he'd talk to you about it, but obviously he didn't. I should've come clean earlier."

Skyler's hand had gone limp. Myra was still holding tight.

"So last night was a setup?" he asked. A dagger had been lodged into his heart.

The rodeo practice. Myra had invited his grandma. Skyler had enjoyed his time with Myra's family. He'd shown Finch a few more chords on the guitar and cheered for Paisley when she'd run barrels. He'd been certain of the way Myra had looked at him in the trailer, just before he'd leaned in to kiss her . . . but it had all been fake? Part of a scheme?

"No," Myra replied with conviction. "Last night didn't have anything to do with the contract. My feelings for you don't have a thing to do with that stupid piece of paper. I wish I hadn't signed it. I'm so sorry, Skyler. I wish I could take it back."

"I don't know what to say." A small voice in his head whispered that this was what happened when people came into his life. It was why he had a hard time trusting. Ever since he'd fallen into the spotlight, it had seemed as though everyone wanted something from him. But he hadn't expected that of Myra.

"Maybe if we'd crossed paths earlier in life, we could've been something . . ." Myra's sentence trailed off. Regardless, it hit Skyler like a ton of bricks.

Could've been something.

Skyler slid his hand from hers, feeling lost. Devastated. For the second time in the past few weeks, the future he'd imagined had been ripped out from underneath him.

Skyler stood, slowly. "I need to go."

"Skyler," she started, but he couldn't take anymore. He needed space to think. He needed to find Cedric. He wanted the hole in his heart to stop bleeding. So he walked out of the barn and drove off.

By the time Skyler arrive at his house, his blood had simmered and then boiled. He parked next to a rental car he assumed was Cedric's and beelined it inside. When he spotted Cedric sitting in his living room, the only thing that stopped him from grabbing Cedric by his collar and ripping him off the couch was the fact that Grandma and Carol sat with him, sipping tea.

"There you are," Cedric greeted Skyler like an old friend. His white teeth glimmered in the fakest smile Skyler had ever seen. "Dorthea and Carol were just telling me about the rodeo last night."

Skyler felt like a snake had entered his home, and he was ready to show the slithering creep to the door.

"Grandma, Carol," Skyler said, keeping his voice even. "Could I have a few minutes alone with Cedric?"

"Of course," Carol replied. She rose to gather her teacup and Dorthea's. "We told him all about those adorable kiddos last night. Didn't we, Dorthea?"

Dorthea, whose gaze had been fixed on her teacup, suddenly beamed brightly. "Oh, yes. They were so cute in their boots and riding their ponies."

"They were." Skyler smiled as his grandma and Carol left the room. When he turned back to Cedric, the smile vanished from Skyler's face. "When were you going to tell me you spoke with Myra?"

Cedric's face slackened. "What do you mean?"

"Cedric," Skyler warned. "I need you to tell me everything. *Right now*. The whole truth. This is the one and only chance you will get." Skyler stared, hoping Cedric could see the fire in his eyes.

Cedric shifted uncomfortably on the couch. "There's not really much to tell. I—"

"Myra told me about the contract," Skyler added.

Cedric stilled. The air was tense enough to break.

"You wouldn't have agreed if I'd told you," Cedric replied. "Besides, they were just pictures, Skyler. And you know better than anyone that the paparazzi were going to find you eventually. This way, we got to control which pictures were released to the press first. We got to feed pictures and stories to the media that helped get you back in good graces with Country Records. We—"

"Stop saying *we*," Skyler interjected. "*We* didn't do anything. I certainly don't remember having a conversation with you in which *we* discussed this plan of yours. But I do remember telling you that I wasn't sure I wanted another contract with Country Records. I also specifically remember saying I needed a break from the music industry and the media."

"Oh, come on now." Cedric waved a hand, brushing aside Skyler's remarks. "You don't mean that. Country Records is the biggest country music label in the world. You think you're just going to give that up?"

"Yeah," Skyler replied easily. And he didn't need to explain anything further to Cedric. What else had his agent done behind his back? He was obviously prioritizing dollar signs over what Skyler needed. The more money Skyler brought in, the bigger Cedric's commissions were. If Skyler didn't sign a new contract with Country Records, that wouldn't be ideal for Cedric's pocketbook.

Cedric slid to the edge of the couch, his elbows on his knees. "I've got us a meeting with the label on Monday. I told them you'd need a thirty percent increase with a new contract. Let's just get through this weekend, and we can reassess on Monday. You can perform at the Country Music Awards tomorrow, and then on Monday—"

"Oh, I will," Skyler replied, and he forced himself to smile. "I'll perform at the CMAs tomorrow, and I'll meet with the label on Monday."

Cedric looked relieved. He sunk back into the couch. "You've finally come to your senses."

"But it will be by myself because you are *fired*."

Cedric's face twisted. "What?" He got to his feet like he'd been launched by a spring. "After all I've done for you?"

"Cedric, you've made a fortune off me, and now I'm wondering what other shenanigans you've pulled behind my back. Even if I had come to an agreement with the label, how in the heck did you think you were going to break the news to me that you'd given my coffee shop away?" How was that supposed to play out? Had Cedric thought Skyler wouldn't notice?

"Oh, for cripes' sake. Do you think I would *give away* one of your businesses?" Cedric's hands went up like he couldn't believe Skyler's ignorance. "I'll show you the contract. It was written up by the label's lawyer. There is a whole lot of legal mumbo jumbo in there that protects you. Basically, for Myra to hold up her end of the contract, she would've had to be responsible for every single photo that was submitted to the media up until the moment you signed a new contract with Country Records. And that is not the case. She barely helped me get a few pictures the first day after you bought the shop. And even then, I had to badger her. Besides, if she took you to court, that contract would never hold up. Do you think I would do that to you?"

Skyler wondered if his head might whirl off his shoulders like a spinning top. Did Cedric think that was a good answer? He'd not only gone behind Skyler's back, but he'd intentionally tricked Myra. He'd taken advantage of her on the day her whole world had fallen apart.

Skyler picked up his hand and pointed to the door. "Get out. *Now.* I don't ever want to see your face again. We are *beyond* done." He was using all his self-restraint not to pummel Cedric in the face.

Cedric roughly ran his hand over his mouth while grumbling a few choice words. "You're going to regret this," he spat. Then he stomped out of the house, slamming the door on his way out.

There were plenty of decisions Skyler had made in his life that he regretted. This was not one of them.

Chapter Twenty-Three

Myra saddled Charm and went for a ride. She meandered the dirt trail that edged the lake and galloped the field on the back side of the pastures, but when she made her way back to the barn, she didn't feel a lick better than when she'd left. The only difference was that her face was tear-streaked and her hair was wind-whipped.

Riding usually fixed everything. At least while she was in the saddle. *Not this time.*

This time, she couldn't stop thinking about how Skyler had looked when she'd told him about the contract. She'd hurt him. Deeply. And she hadn't been ready for the way that would affect her. It was like being thrown from the saddle, hitting the ground, and having the wind knocked from her lungs. She wasn't sure when she'd breathe again.

After brushing out Charm, Myra headed home. When she pulled around the back of Perkup, she hoped to see Skyler's car. But the gravel alley was empty. Myra parked her truck and got out.

The kids were at their dad's, and the coffee shop was closed. Becca had covered the rest of the day when Myra had taken off to talk with Skyler.

Taking a deep breath, she turned toward her mom's house, wanting the comfort of a warm hug and a shoulder to lean on. She also knew it was time to tell her mom the truth.

"Momma?" Myra called as she stepped through the back door. The kitchen smelled like Judy's fried pork chops, but Myra had no appetite.

"In the living room," Judy called back. "You hungry, sweetie? I got a whole ton of leftovers I put in the fridge." Judy was sitting in her favorite recliner. *Jeopardy!* played on the television, and she had a crossword puzzle in her hand. When she saw Myra, she dropped the crossword puzzle to her lap. "Sweet baby Jesus. What happened?"

"It's okay, Mom. No one is hurt." Myra knew what her face looked like. Puffy and snotty. "Physically, I mean." That wasn't true. Her heart felt like it was being crushed.

"Is it the kids?" Judy hopped out of the recliner like she hadn't just had a hip replacement.

"The kids are good. It's me. I need to tell you something."

"Spit it out, sweetie. You're going to give an old woman a heart attack. And I didn't survive all that silly physical therapy just to croak now." Judy stepped toward Myra and offered her hands.

Myra took them and looked her mom straight in the eyes. "I lied to you and the kids. To everyone, really."

Judy's brow furrowed. "About what?"

"About the shop."

Judy gave Myra's hands a little shake. "I said spit it out, child. Tell me what happened."

Myra took a deep breath. When she released it, the truth came with. "Skyler isn't my partner. He owns the shop. He bought it when I let it go into foreclosure. I don't own it anymore."

Judy's eyes bulged. On the TV behind her, one of the *Jeopardy!* contestants said, "What is the deepest hole in the world?" Myra felt like he was referring to the hole she'd dug herself into.

"How did that happen?" Judy asked. "How'd you go into fore-closure? I thought everything was fine. You loaned money to me for my surgery." Judy gasped like she'd suddenly seen a ghost, and it absolutely pained Myra. This was what she'd been avoiding. She never wanted her mother to feel guilty for accepting her help. "You lent me money when you were struggling to pay bills?"

"You needed the surgery, Mom. I wasn't going to let you go any longer without it. And that's not the only reason I was behind on bills. I thought I was okay. I thought I could get my finances back on track. I just couldn't do it fast enough."

"Myra," Judy said, sternly. "If you *ever* need my help, you dang well better tell me so. That's what mommas are for. Right? You know that."

Tears welled in Myra's eyes. "I do know that, Mom. And I wish I would've just told you." A tear slipped down her cheek. Judy reached up and brushed it away.

"I'm here for you. You're here for me. We're both here for Paisley and Finch. That's what family is for." Judy squeezed Myra's hands, reminding Myra of the words she'd said to her own daughter just yesterday. *You can tell me anything. Anytime. I'm serious. If you're hurting, I want to know so I can help. I'm here for you, no matter what.*

"I didn't want you to worry, and I didn't want to disappoint you," Myra admitted. "And I didn't want you to delay your surgery."

"Honey, you don't concern yourself with what I worry about or don't worry about. And don't you dare think I'd be disappointed in you. I am so very proud of you for all your accomplishments, for the woman and mother you are. You make me proud every day. One stumbling block is not going to change that. A million stumbling blocks wouldn't change how proud I am of you." Judy pulled her into a hug. "I love you so very much. And if you'd told me you were in trouble, I would've figured out a way to help you. Okay? I could've sold my house . . . or baked a thousand pies to sell at the farmers market . . . or hosted a million Tupperware parties. Believe me, I'd have figured something out."

Myra closed her eyes, listening to all the ways Judy would've come to her rescue. She let herself lean on her mom, take in her warm hug, recognize that they were alike in so many ways. They'd each do anything to protect those they loved. No matter the cost. And Myra was grateful to have been brought up by such a strong, loving woman.

"Thanks, Mom. I love you," Myra said into Judy's shoulder, knowing it didn't matter how old she was. Getting a big hug from her mom was like being wrapped in a warm, fuzzy blanket. It was the reminder she needed right at this very moment: she didn't *have* to do everything on her own.

Judy squeezed Myra tight one more time before ushering her to the couch. "Now, you sit and relax while I make you something to eat."

Myra didn't argue. She curled into the couch and mindlessly watched *Jeopardy!* as Judy clanked away in the kitchen. In a few minutes, Judy came back with a steaming plate of pork chops, scalloped potatoes, and creamed corn. She set it on Myra's lap.

"Thanks, Momma." Myra wasn't hungry, but she put a huge spoonful of potatoes in her mouth. The cheese and starch would make her feel better.

"So, are you going to tell me what's going on with Skyler, then?" Judy asked as Myra chewed.

Myra swallowed. "He's paying me a salary. A really good salary. And he's not charging me rent for the apartment. I'm saving up and want to buy the shop back from him when he's ready to sell."

Judy tilted her head and stared at her from the recliner. "I wasn't talking about the shop."

Myra forked a piece of pork chop into her mouth. "What do you mean?" She chewed. She knew perfectly well what her mother meant, but she had no intention of getting into that subject. There was no sense in talking about a relationship that couldn't be.

"Anyone with eyes and ears can see that the two of you are crazy about each other."

Myra closed her eyes and stopped chewing. She wanted that to be the truth. She also knew there were too many hurdles to make it work between the two of them. And Hurdle Number One consisted of the fact that she'd lied to Skyler.

"Mom, I really screwed up." Before she could tell Judy about the contract she'd signed, Judy raised a single finger.

"Sweetie, life is made up of a whole lot of trial and error. I've lived it. I know. I've made plenty of errors. But if you don't go back and try again, you'll never get where you want to be. Nobody is perfect. We're all going to make mistakes. It's how you move on after a mistake that's important. Now, you don't have to tell me what happened between you and Skyler. I can see you're upset. But can you tell me what you'd like to happen?"

For Skyler to forgive her. To see his bright smile again. To laugh with him over a cup of coffee and watch him teach her kids to play guitar. To be with him the first time his grandma saw the shop. To have him in her life—every day.

When Myra didn't reply out loud, Judy said, "You need to go talk to him."

"What would I say?"

"That you're falling in love with him."

Myra laughed, stunned, and nearly choked on a piece of pork chop. "Mom, that's crazy. I've only known him for two weeks."

"It's not crazy. It's love. I can see it on your face." Judy offered a soft smile. "It's only crazy if you don't make your feelings known."

Myra sat there, blinking. She thought about what she'd said to Skyler earlier tonight. She'd tried to tell him how she felt, but once she'd seen the disappointment on his face, her words had gotten jumbled. They hadn't come out right.

She'd told him that they could've worked out if they'd met at a different time in life. She'd unintentionally pushed him away without making her true feelings known. She'd thrown a wall up to shield her heart.

I'm not protecting my heart. I'm stopping myself from falling in love.

She was her own hurdle. And if she didn't tell Skyler how she truly felt, she'd never know if they could be something. If she didn't take the risk, she'd lose the chance. And she wanted a chance at love. With Skyler.

Chapter Twenty-Four

That evening, Skyler chartered a private plane to Nashville. The whole way there, he thought about what Myra had said. Her words churned over and over in his head, but her last comment grated at him. *If we'd crossed paths earlier in life, we could've been something.* She'd said it like there wasn't a chance they could be something now. Like everything he'd been feeling for her, every beautiful experience they'd shared, hadn't been enough. That bothered him the most.

It bothered him more than the secret she'd kept from him. At least that, he could understand. It hurt, but he knew Cedric had tricked her. Cedric had caught Myra in a corner and taken advantage of her when she was vulnerable. But even then—even when the coffee shop was on the line—she'd chosen to put Skyler's needs before her own.

And who was he to judge anyone for keeping a secret?

He'd been pretending to be someone he wasn't for years. He still was. Even today, after all that he'd been through, he was still following a path that didn't represent his true self.

As he walked the red carpet the next day, dressed in a designer suit the label had picked out for him, Skyler's mind wandered to the conversation he'd had with Myra on the water tower. She'd asked him *why* he sang country music, and he'd told her it was because of the stories in the lyrics, the truth behind the words. Yet he'd allowed so many people to hijack his truth. He'd buried his own passions and ignored his gut for far too long.

Now, there was only one set of ears that needed to hear his truth, so five minutes before going on stage, Skyler grabbed his phone. He called Myra. The call rang and rang, and when it went to voicemail, Skyler's heart dropped. The only thing he could think to say was, "Please turn on your TV. Watch the Country Music Awards. I need you to hear what I have to say."

As he hung up, Skyler turned to his band and asked if they'd be willing to make a last-minute song change. When they all agreed, Skyler slung his guitar strap over his head and walked out onto a dark stage. His band members took their positions behind instruments and microphones. The packed audience applauded.

As the clapping quieted and the spotlight found him, nerves rolled in Skyler's stomach. The show's production crew assessed him quizzically. He was holding an acoustic guitar—not the electric guitar they expected for "Dirt Roads and Diesel."

Skyler wrapped a hand around the microphone and looked at the closest camera. "Tonight, I'm going to play something different than what was planned. It's a song I wrote many years ago, but it means something different to me now than it did back then. And that's because of a very special person who came into my life."

A low hum sputtered through the audience. A few of the production crew ran backstage like something was on fire, but Skyler continued. "This person taught me a lot in a short period of time. She reminded me to listen to my heart, that passion will always trump circumstance, and she showed me what true love looks like."

A trickle of sweat ran down his back. He was laying it all out there. Even if Myra wasn't watching the live show, she'd certainly see it after the fact. His speech would make the rounds on every entertainment platform. He didn't care, as long as it made its way to her.

"Tonight, I'm going to sing 'This Should've Been a Love Song.' Originally, when I wrote this ballad, it was about a love that never was. It was a sad story about a broken heart. But I recently rewrote the last verse. And now, I want to dedicate this song to Myra. She's my inspiration. She's the reason I had to change my song."

Skyler glanced down at his guitar. His fingers found the strings, and he strummed a chord. After a few beats, his band joined in. Music filled the stage. Lyrics, words, and a story sat in Skyler's chest, and he was ready to send them out into the world. He hoped they meant as much to Myra as they meant to him.

He sang his heart out. Especially the last verse . . . which spoke of a love he couldn't live without.

At the end of Skyler's performance, the audience exploded into applause. They were still clapping as he made his way backstage and into his dressing room. Skyler threw his guitar on the couch and grabbed his phone, looking for Myra's name, hoping she'd called. A million texts and calls had come through while he was on stage. Before he could find Myra's name, he received a video call from his grandma.

Skyler picked up, and two smiling faces beamed at him. Dorthea clasped her hands together under her chin. Carol was sitting right next to her, just as thrilled.

"Oh, that was so beautiful," Dorthea cooed, her eyes glistening. "I love how you changed your song just for Myra. Now it truly is a love song. And you know how I love a love song." She shrugged in adoration.

Skyler smiled. "I do, Grandma. I'm so glad you liked it." At least he'd made his grandma and Carol happy. Now, if only the song had made its way to Myra—and touched her heart as well.

"So, Myra made it there?" Carol asked, her eyebrows raised in anticipation.

Skyler cocked his head. "Made it where?"

Carol looked confused. "To Nashville. To the CMAs."

"Myra's here?" Skyler nearly dropped the phone.

Carol and Dorthea nodded vigorously. "She came to the house last night looking for you," Carol said. "Dorthea and I had a heart-to-heart with her."

"She really cares about you," Dorthea added seriously.

"And she really wanted to talk with you in person," Carol said. "Your grandma and I decided it couldn't wait, so we got her a plane ticket for this morning. And we called that nice Blake Shelton friend of yours. He said he'd take care of Myra and get her into the show."

Skyler's insides exploded. Myra was here? *Where?*

"I've got to find her." The words spilled out of his mouth.

"Yes, go find her, my love!" Dorthea said. Carol repeated her sentiments.

"I love you guys." Skyler sent an air kiss toward the phone and ended the call. Dorthea and Carol returned the gesture before the screen went black.

Skyler ran out of his dressing room, calling Myra's phone as he did. He sprinted down the hall, not sure where he was running, but he'd burst back out on stage if he had to. Would he sound crazy if he started to shout her name?

On the third ring, he spotted her. Myra had just turned the corner, appearing at the other end of the hall with a security guard. She was dressed in a black satin gown that cascaded to the floor. Her hair fell in waves over her shoulders. She looked like a princess . . . no, she looked like a queen. Skyler stopped, afraid his eyes were playing tricks on him.

When Myra's gaze met his, her crimson lips fell open. She said his name, though he could only read her lips. Another band was on stage, and music filled the hall. Drums and bass vibrated through his chest. Skyler couldn't tell the difference between the music and the beat of his heart.

Then Myra grasped her skirt to hold it out of her way, exposing the black cowboy boots beneath, and ran toward Skyler. He ran too, meeting her halfway and wrapping her in his arms.

"You're here," he breathed, his face pressed into her hair. "I can't believe you're here."

Myra unraveled her arms from his neck and took his face in her hands. Her blue eyes glistened, full of tears. He hoped they were happy ones. "You changed your song for me."

He nodded, keeping his hands pressed tightly around her waist, not wanting a sliver of space to separate them. "You heard it?"

She blinked, pushing back tears. "I was in the audience. I heard it loud and clear."

His heart bound in his chest. Myra had heard his lyrics—his confession of love. He had laid his heart open for her to see. "I had to rewrite it. The lyrics didn't make sense to me anymore. I had to change it . . . for you. You turned that into a love song, Myra. Our love song."

She smiled brightly at him. "It's the most beautiful love song I've ever heard. I wanted to run to you on stage to kiss you, but I didn't want to share our moment—this moment—with anyone but you." The hall was empty except for the security guard. And when Skyler gave the guard a nod, he disappeared.

Now there was no audience. No cameras. It was just the two of them.

"You know, you could've called me and saved me a heart attack." He grinned, trying to make a joke out of the truth.

Myra laughed. She let her hands fall from Skyler's face to his chest. "I couldn't do that. I needed to talk to you in person. To tell you something face to face."

"And what did you want to tell me?" He held her stare.

"That I got scared," she replied. "Last night, I couldn't put my feelings into words, and I pushed you away when I thought you were going to break my heart. After you left, I realized we'd never have a chance if I didn't share my heart fully. And that it's okay to be scared and still take the risk of telling you how I feel. Because the risk is worth the reward." Her gaze flitted over his face like a soft breeze. "I want to be with you, Skyler. I want to kiss you and cook for you and take you to family suppers. I want to share every piece of life with you. The good, the bad. All of it."

"Ditto," Skyler replied, and the smile that hit Myra's face pushed him to add, "I'm falling in love with you."

Her eyes widened, and Skyler knew the risk *he* was taking. He also knew he was done with secrets.

"Actually, that's a lie. I'm there. I love you, Myra."

Dizzy with emotion, Skyler worried she wouldn't say it back, but Myra instantly went up on her tiptoes, getting as close to his lips as possible.

"I want us to live out our own love song. I love you too, Sky." Then she sealed her words with a kiss that deserved a standing ovation.

And there, in that empty hall, Skyler had no doubt Myra would inspire a million more love songs. He was ready to write them. More than that, he couldn't wait to sing them for her.

Epilogue

ONE WEEK LATER

A long table was situated on the back wall of Perkup, filled with all the makings of Sunday supper. Aunt Joyce's sliced ham. Mom's creamed corn. Hazel's homemade buttered buns. Kat's slow-cooker mashed potatoes. Myra stood before the feast and added a green bean casserole. She situated the steaming pan onto a couple of hot plates, reveling in the murmurs of happy conversation behind her. Her whole family filled the coffee shop—her kids, parents, grandpa, aunts, uncles, cousins, nieces, nephews, and close family friends. Their presence made her heart sing. Usually, Sunday supper was at Joyce and Gene's house, but today was extra special, and Myra had wanted to host the event at Perkup. They had much to celebrate. Plus, there were two very special guests coming for the feast today.

Finch raced over and placed a stack of paper plates on the far end of the table. Paisley strode in behind him with a basket of silverware.

"There, Momma," Finch said, enthusiastically, and ran off like he had another important task to complete. It probably involved playing tag outside with his cousins.

Paisley added the basket of silverware to the table. "You need anything else, Mom?" She was still wearing her apron, and the sight of it made Myra smile. Paisley had helped Myra make the green bean casserole this morning. She'd also helped bake the pies for today's event. Last night, Myra and Paisley had whipped up half a dozen chocolate pies in Skyler's kitchen alongside Dorthea and Carol. While the four of them had baked, Skyler had taken Finch fishing in his fancy new boat. Finch had almost died of excitement.

"Nope. I think we're good." Myra kissed her daughter on the forehead. "Thanks for your help, baby."

Paisley smiled. A genuine expression. Not one of those snarky teenage smirks. "You're welcome." She untied her apron and pulled it over her head. "I'm going to go get my guitar so I can practice a little."

Myra gave Paisley a nod and watched her daughter nearly skip away. Paisley and Finch had been practicing a song with Skyler. The three of them were going to play for the family today. The kids were both eager to do so. Myra couldn't wait to hear their guitars and voices mingle together.

Just then, a warm hand settled on her lower back. She turned and got caught in Skyler's amber eyes.

"Hey, partner," he whispered with a smile that made her want to kiss him.

Myra bit her lower lip, containing herself for the time being. "Hey, partner," she repeated, loving the sound of the word.

Yesterday, they'd made it official. Skyler and Myra had gone to the bank and signed a contract they could both feel good about. They were now fifty-fifty partners in Perkup. Skyler had tried to gift the shop to Myra, but she wouldn't have it. She didn't want a gift. She wanted to be equals . . . in business and in love. And that was exactly what she had now. They'd agreed on the financials and a payment plan, and now Skyler and Myra were partners. *Real* partners. From now on, their lives would be intertwined. And Myra couldn't be happier about that. Especially because she knew Skyler was sticking around for good.

After the Country Music Awards, Skyler had met with Country Records and passed on a new contract. He'd also told them he'd keep his mouth shut about how they'd treated him if his band members were given a hefty severance. After they came to an agreement that would take care of his band for years, Skyler was officially done with Country Records. However, he wasn't done with country music. He just wanted to pursue a different path. Instead of living in the spotlight, Skyler wanted to write songs. He wanted to craft lyrics and paint stories for other singers to play on stages around the world.

"Carol called," Skyler said. "She and Grandma are just leaving the house."

Myra wrapped her hand in Skyler's. "Are you excited? Worried?"

"A little of both."

"Well, I'm excited. For both you and Dorthea." Myra squeezed his hand. "Everything will be just fine. Even if Dorthea doesn't remember being here, she's coming for a big family dinner. We'll create new experiences. And who can have a bad day when mashed potatoes and chocolate pie are involved?"

Skyler leaned over and kissed Myra on her forehead. His lips lingered there for a few heartbeats. "Thanks for being here with me and for pulling all this together."

"I wouldn't have it any other way."

"I'm going to go wait for Carol and Grandma outside."

Myra gave his hand another squeeze, and then Skyler headed through the crowded shop and out the front door. Once he was outside, Myra gave a few loud claps, getting everyone's attention. "All right, Dorthea and Carol are on their way. After they get settled, we'll eat."

Mom and Aunt Joyce stood near the counter, chatting. When Myra made her announcement, they set down their mugs, rounded up Grandpa Vern, and escorted him to the front window. Myra took off her apron and joined them.

"You look so handsome, Grandpa." Myra straightened Vern's bow tie and smoothed his sweater vest.

"Not as handsome as I did sixty years ago," Vern replied, seeming nervous as he looked out the window.

"I beg to differ," Myra replied, but she understood her grandpa's nerves.

"She's a very nice lady, Dad." Judy rubbed Vern's shoulder and gave him a little hug.

"It'll be good for you to reconnect." Joyce squeezed his other arm.

"Mom would want you to," Judy added, and Myra's eyes went misty.

Earlier that week, after Skyler and Myra had gotten home from Nashville, Skyler had brought the picture of his grandma to the shop. Myra had showed it to her grandpa. She'd hoped he'd have some insight as to who the owners had been at the time the photo was taken. She hadn't expected her grandpa to recognize the woman in the photograph.

"Dorthea," he'd said, barely above a whisper. "I remember taking this picture."

"*You* took this?" Myra had said in disbelief. Skyler stood beside her, his mouth open in shock.

Vern had proceeded to explain that Dorthea and he had met that day. Vern had been a groomsman in an Army buddy's wedding. Dorthea had been a childhood friend of the bride. Vern and Dorthea had danced the night away across the wooden barn floor. It was where they fell in love. After the wedding, they dated for a few months, but at the end of the summer, Vern had been drafted overseas. They wrote letters but slowly drifted apart, ultimately finding different paths. That next year, Vern had met the love of his life, Myra's Grandma Barbara.

"Barbie would want me to be Dorthea's friend," Vern said confidently. "Especially because she's going through the same thing my dear Barbie battled." Grandpa personally knew the struggles of dementia. He also knew how to navigate those struggles. Which was why both Myra and Skyler had thought reintroducing Dorthea and Vern would be good for them both.

Carol parked her car in front of the shop. Skyler opened the passenger door and helped his grandma out. Dorthea looked adorable in pink capris and a white blouse. She beamed up at Skyler, as she always did. He and Carol escorted her to the front door.

When they entered, Finch and Paisley gave Dorthea hugs. She giggled at the attention, and Myra loved the way her kids made Dorthea light up.

"Come on, Grandpa." Myra offered her arm. Vern took it, and they walked to Skyler and his grandma.

"Dorthea, I have someone I'd like to introduce you to," Myra said.

Dorthea looked a little surprised, but Vern offered his hand. She took it.

"Hi, Dorthea. I'm Vernon Richards. I'm not sure if you recognize me with all the wrinkles I've earned over the years, but we met a long, long time ago. I was a groomsman in Suzie Lee's wedding. It's so very nice to see you again."

Myra held her breath. She could tell Skyler was doing the same.

Dorthea's surprise melted into recognition. "Suzie Lee's wedding? The one in the barn with the dancing and the four-tier cake?" She gave a little gasp. Then she looked at Skyler. He reassured her with a smile. Dorthea looked back at Vern. "Oh, I remember you, Vernon. You and your fancy feet. Can you still do a two-step?"

Grandpa chuckled, and Myra tried not to cry from pure joy.

"Sure can," Vern said, and Dorthea's eyes sparkled. "Are you hungry, Dorthea? Because my girls made enough food to feed the whole town. Can I show you to your seat?"

"I'd like that," Dorthea said. She patted Skyler's arm, and he let her go. Vern and Dorthea teetered off together toward the table packed with food.

Skyler and Myra looked at each other, amazed, before Skyler pulled Myra into a bear hug. He kissed her temple. "That makes me so happy."

"Me too." Myra's cheeks hurt from smiling. "Oh, that reminds me. I have a surprise for you." She broke their embrace, grabbed his hand, and pulled Skyler behind the counter.

Myra opened a drawer and pulled out the black-and-white photo, which was now in a wooden frame. She turned to Skyler. "I had Dorthea's picture framed. I thought we could hang it in the shop. *Our* shop."

Skyler circled an arm around Myra's waist. "I can't imagine it anywhere else."

As Skyler pulled her close, Myra knew her path had been meant to cross his. Fate had brought them together, but opening their hearts had sealed their destiny. They were an unexpected combination—like the blackberry-maple latte. Sour at first, then unbelievably sweet to the end.

"Love you, Sky," Myra whispered.

Then he kissed her, tasting of coffee and bliss and sugar and love.

The Next Maple Bay Book

WANT TO READ EVAN & VAL'S LOVE STORY?

Get the next book in the series: Matched in Maple Bay!

Stay in touch & never miss a new release ~ Sign-up for Brittney Joy's newsletter:
http://www.brittneyjoybooks.com/newsletter

Thank You

Thank you for reading *Country Stars in Maple Bay*! I hope this story touched your heart the way it touched mine. If you enjoyed it, I'd love it if you would post your honest review anywhere you purchased your book. Reviews help me understand what stories readers enjoy. They also help me decide what to write next. Your review is greatly appreciated! And if you loved it, tell your friends! The best way to spread the word about a book is through word of mouth!

Never miss a new release ~ Join Brittney Joy's newsletter:
http://www.brittneyjoybooks.com/newsletter

Chocolate Pie Recipe

- 2 cups cold milk

- 2 packages (4 serving sizes each) of chocolate flavored instant pudding & pie filling

- 1 tub (8 oz) Cool Whip topping, thawed

- 1 Oreo pie crust (6 oz)

- 1 cup of crushed M&Ms (red & green are fun to use at Christmas time)

- Optional: additional topping of your choice (toasted coconut, chocolate flakes, sprinkles, or fruit)

1. Pour the cold milk into a large mixing bowl and add the dry pudding mixes. Beat with a wire whisk for a few min-

utes or until well mixed.

2. Gently stir in 1 ½ cups of the Cool Whip.

3. Set aside a ¼ cup of the crushed M&Ms. Stir the remaining (3/4 cup) crushed candy into the pudding mix.

4. Pour the pudding mix into the Oreo crust and smooth with the back of a spoon. Top with the rest of the Cool Whip (or save the Cool Whip and put a dollop on each pie piece as it is served).

5. Sprinkle with the rest of the M&Ms (and/or use additional toppings such as toasted coconut, chocolate flakes, sprinkles, or fruit).

6. Serve immediately or chill in the fridge until ready to eat.

7. Enjoy!

Matched in Maple Bay

A Maple Bay Novel, Book 4

They aren't looking to rebuild a love from the past, but this renovation uncovers more than either of them expected.

Valerie Ricci is determined to nail together the pieces of her career after a messy divorce from her husband and co-host. Things are looking up when she lands her own fixer-upper TV show where she will design & renovate old homes across the country. It's her chance to prove to everyone she can pull in ratings by herself. Except the first house she must renovate is Evan Weston's—the man who broke her heart twenty years ago.

Evan Weston loves small town life, quiet evenings with his horses, and Sunday dinners with his close-knit family. He's worked hard to make a comfortable life for himself and his seventeen-year-old daughter, Issy—who he'd do anything for. Which is why he's so conflicted when Issy surprises him with a camera crew and an ex-girlfriend he hasn't seen in nearly two decades.No one else has any idea Valerie and Evan dated, and they plan to keep it that way.

But as they tear down the walls of his old farmhouse, they can't help but uncover new layers of their shared history. Will they build a new connection on an old foundation, or is this one restoration that isn't built for a second chance?

Get Your Copy Today!

Also by Brittney Joy

Sweet Romance Books:
Rescued in Maple Bay
Starting Over in Maple Bay
Second Chance in Maple Bay
Country Stars in Maple Bay
Matched in Maple Bay
Christmas in Silver Leaf Falls
Sincerely Not Yours

Red Rock Ranch Series: Young Adult Contemporary
Lucy's Chance
Showdown
Rodeo Daze

The OverRuled Series: Young Adult Fantasy
OverRuled
OverRun
OverThrown

Checkout all books here:

www.brittneyjoybooks.com

About the Author

Brittney Joy writes sweet stories full of hope, heart, and happily-ever-afters. She and her family live in their own piece of heaven in the Oregon countryside. They stay busy with their menagerie of silly horses, cackling chickens, wooly sheep, two very naughty goats, a scheming cat, and an adorable dog. When Brittney isn't writing, she's riding or reading. And she wishes she could do all three at the same time.

www.brittneyjoybooks.com